boldface names

boldface names

shinan govani

HarperCollins Publishers Ltd

Boldface Names

Published by HarperCollins Publishers Ltd.

This is a lighthearted work of fiction. The author has drawn inspiration, in part, from his experiences as a society columnist; however, except where the names of real people are used, the characters are imaginary, as is the story.

First edition

HarperCollins Publishers Ltd
2 Bloor Street East, 20th Floor
Toronto, Ontario, Canada
M4W 1A8

www.harpercollins.ca

Library and Archives Canada Cataloguing in Publication
Govani, Shinan
Boldface names : a novel / Shinan Govani.
ISBN 978-1-55468-319-2
I. Title.
PS8613.O972B65 2009 C813'.6 C2008-907930-2

Boldface Names is printed on Ancient Forest Friendly paper, made with 100% post-consumer waste

Printed in Canada
DWF 9 8 7 6 5 4 3 2 1

For Mummy and Daddy,
with love

"I'd hate to take a bite out of you.
You're a cookie full of arsenic."
—*Sweet Smell of Success* (1957)

1

Secrets and Wives

Exactly three months to the day after they got married, Ravi and Rory consummated their union.

"I'm so sorry it took so long," Ravi told his wife of approximately ninety days after enacting their breathless and incontrovertible answer to the Terry Fox Run. "It's just I've been so busy, what with the social season and the column and, oh, the travelling! Honestly, sweetheart, I jet-set so much, I can't even be bothered to steal the toiletries from hotels anymore."

"Stop apologizing, buster," Rory said, her glistening eyes reminding him, just a little, of the smoky dark flatware he'd seen at the annual Brazilian Ball funder. Come to think of it, her hair was as fine as the font on the invite he'd just received for that Louis Vuitton party in New York City. "We said we'd keep it a secret," she continued, firm. "Even if it's keeping us apart. I gave you my word."

At which point, the bride that dare not speak its name mistakenly knocked to the floor a book that had been sitting most tenuously on Ravi's bedside table next to a miniature skyline of all the latest magazines, a doodle pad he kept for story ideas that may have stirred in his dreams, and, most importantly, a sniffle-stopping supersized carton of Emergen-C. Conscientious gal that she was, Rory leaned over to pick up what she'd dropped, all the while hiding her privileged parts under the sheets like she was Julia Roberts in bed with Hugh Grant in *Notting Hill.* It was a prized copy of Evelyn Waugh's *Vile Bodies* that had toppled over.

"Isn't this the one with the Bright Young Things and the gossip columnist?"

"I think I prefer the term *social archivist,*" he devil-may-cared, yawning nonchalantly.

"Well, you would," said the lateral-thinking, sinuously voiced, marionette-limbed woman in his bed. "Always talking about something by referring to something else. You really should go to metaphor rehab, Ravi . . . or, like, a Betty Ford for euphemisms."

"You're clever, Rory, but I don't like you bossing me around on our ostensible honeymoon," he come-backed as she turned, giving a vista of her beautiful back.

Becoming coy, and a tadish serious, while running a hand through his remarkably well-follicled mane, he pilfered a smile away from her. Then he grovelled. "So, we're sticking to the plan, right? Nobody can know that I'm married."

"Least of all . . . to a woman," she fumbled.

"I have a reputation, after all," he spelled out.

"Are you going to the party tonight for Dou?" his feminine foil went on, changing the subject with miraculous finesse. "They say that Canadian girl who's on *90210* might show up. And Ellen Page too."

"She's come a long way since *Juno*, and she has a new tattoo," piped Ravi, showing off a near-rabbinical knowledge of anything and everything celebrity.

"And Kim Cattrall, who doesn't have a new tattoo but does still have a boyfriend," returned Rory, who, despite her business degree, or because of it, could go toe to toe with her husband any day on this-or-that trivia. "It's that same boil-toy. That chef guy who used to mine the stoves here in Toronto. And Ivanka Trump. For some reason, she's going to be there. Or maybe it's Ivana."

"And," Ravi continued, "the son—or maybe it's a daughter—of the prime minister of an African country I can't remember, but it's one that's been in the news lately, I'm fairly certain."

"Sudan?"

"No."

"Oh.

"So," she started up again, "are you doing Dou's party tonight? Doesn't he give you three-hundred-dollar comp haircuts? Isn't it Dou or die time, especially with his last salon going spectacularly bust, and all that tax evasion stuff . . ."

"Alleged evasion. Anyway, can't. Have to work." Ravi peered at Rory with Emmy Award–worthy lament. Even though he was emotionally parsimonious by nature, this woman managed to bring out his ostentatious side, feelings-wise.

"Well, elementary, my dear Warhol," she said.

"No humble hairdresser-hosted meet-and-greets for me tonight," he continued, tickling her toes. "Have to go to an Italian three-course disguised as an intellectual track meet to see what the smart set is wearing these days. After all the Shania Twain scoopage last week, my editors feel like I need some meat and spuds in the column. Some uptown to go with the downtown and the no-town.

"Plus," he stage-whispered, "Lord Ivory might just be there."

"I can't believe this is your job!" she cried.

Indeed, it was. As had once been said about the preternaturally gifted gadfly—by a grade-A social climber, no less—a party without Ravi was "like a salade niçoise without the tuna."

"You remember what Gore Vidal so famously said, don't you?" she then asked, giving good lash and a long, tortuous sideways glance. "He said, 'Every time a friend of mine succeeds, a little part of me dies.'"

"Well," Ravi said with derring-do, drawing her closer, "it's a pretty good thing I'm more than just a friend."

Sometime later, Ravi rose from the bed, leaving his missus to gum-chew like one of those ballplayers in *A League of Their Own.* Rory slipped on the Aviator sunglasses that had until then, even throughout their torrid lovemaking, sat like a tiara on her well-proportioned head. Crossing his own hands behind his back—much like Prince Philip, a sort of James Brolin to the Queen of England, otherwise known as Helen Mirren—he steered quietly toward the shower.

"Really, Ravi," his sated wife yelled after him, "I can't believe this is your actual job!"

"Some days," Ravi chuckled from his daily baptism, "neither can I."

2

Breaking the Ice

"Could I have a glass of water?" Ravi asked, wondering idly why Canadians such as himself were so pathologically polite when requesting or, more likely, begging for their beverages. At parties in New York City or Miami or whatnottown, most people seemed to summon, "Glass of water" with maybe, but only if they felt like it, or if Jupiter was in their moon, an extra ladle of "please."

Sure, gestured the weary waiter. He looked familiar, in the way that all wait staff seemed to look familiar to Ravi, the professional party-plunger.

Thank you, Ravi motioned as he deftly poured a packet of Emergen-C into a tall, clean glass of nothingness. Oh, yes, it was just like Studio 54 right here in the twenty-first-century party circuit—except that all the powder in his life was orange.

Studio 54 it might not have been, but Chapter 11 did seem to be making a murmur. Everyone inside this sumptuous house belonging to that fantastic, fate-tempting, in-the-news mogul,

Lord Ivory, and his gifted, invidious, quite possibly viperish wife, Lady Ivory, was thinking it. You couldn't help it, though you'd dare not say it. (The word *house,* by the way, is used at this point in the same way that people such as Paul Allen or, say, Valentino like to downplay their gargantuan sea vessels—complete with helipads and cinemas and patisseries—by referring to them, simply and probably reverse-grandiosely, as "boats." Or the way rich people, especially after the recession, like to call themselves "comfortable.")

I should have ordered hot water, he quipped to himself, adding to the ongoing editorial in his head.

The party tonight was in honour of the second anniversary, or possibly the third, of a cult periodical with a right-wing bent reserved chiefly for people who become visibly aroused at the mere skirt-squeak of that ever-nostril-flaring Ann Coulter. Or wish nothing more than to be spiritually breast-fed in the matriarchal bosom of Margaret Thatcher. Ravi had arrived just minutes earlier, entering mistakenly through the servants' quarters, where he was groped, briefly and not altogether unpleasantly, by two guard dogs.

He had been invited to this gaseous orb of lower-tax-inclined eggheads at the Italian three-course dinner he'd attend the night before. The blustering editor of the periodical—a Pillsbury Doughboy pundit of some acclaim, one who lived in a merciful world without grey—had zeroed in on him there and bequeathed an invite on the spot.

"Write it up," he'd said. "Just don't tell anyone I asked you to."

And so he had given his thanks, taken the deets, and gone

home and put the invite in one of five transparent coloured folders he kept on his work desk. All of them were precisely labelled. There was cherry red for High Party Importance (those with big celebrity potential, in other words), coral for Mid-to-High Party Importance (those sort of soirees that were likely to reap good gift bags, and a nice spread, but whose guest list was TBD), citrus for Parties with Potential for Society/Beau Monde/Cultural Elite Fodder (parties that probably only mattered to a few hundred people, but a few hundred of the Right People), bright yellow for Only If Really Desperate Parties (parties that were likely to attract various crashers, arrivistes, and bottom-feeders but were still invaluable for him to attend if it happened to be a slow week in the social goings-on), and, finally, sea-foam green for—and this really was critical—Not So Important Parties but Not a Bad Idea to Attend for Political Purposes (parties that weren't all that hot in the scheme of things but that Ravi was inclined to attend because he owed something to the organizer/publicist/host/sponsor involved or he expected to owe something sometime soon because he fully anticipated to be asking them for a favour on a whole other matter in the near, not-so-near, or distant future).

He'd put the invite for the party at the home of Lord and Lady Ivory in the citrus folder.

"Business or pleasure tonight?" asked the tomb-breathed host of a TV show, stopping Ravi to show off teeth that today came studded with one standalone poppy seed. If this was high school, and he was a she, this guy would be one of those Heathers you couldn't shake.

"My pleasure is my business," Ravi replied with a premeditated carelessness, giving the miserabilist a small salute and moving right along.

The pad, located in an impeachable hood in the Canadian metropolis of Toronto, was all big bucks and mortar, situated on the very street where Prince, the Purple One, had laid down his head at night when he was altogether too briefly wedded to a local girl on the hunt for pop-star husband-prey. It was the kind of house where an oil likeness of Winston Churchill presides over the drawing room, the drapes cost more than the regular upkeep of Joan Collins's wig inventory, the library is oval, the flushing is first rate, and there are wings.

Ravi looked around the room, his own mental YouTube snapping up images that might come in handy for his daily column in the *National Mirror,* a broadsheet that firmly believed in both reportage *and* décolletage. At this sort of shindig it was important, he'd found, to make like an expert escape artist and play the game of being wholly present and visible but at the same time apart.

There, he noted, near the buffet, was a well-known woman with a tidy Jane Goodall ponytail talking to an equally well-known woman with a distinctly Suze Orman overtan, wide-angle beam, slightly protruding paunch, and pugnacious tongue. Both of them were charter members of the intelligentsia, and the latter had been very good at spreading the rumour about herself that she was in Mensa. The former was torn between her love for a famous atheist and her marriage to a lactose-intolerant born-again. Over there, underneath a Peter Doig painting of a canoe, stood a man—one of alleged letters and clogged arteries—who gave off the vibe of someone who needs a lot of Me-Time and looked something like the substitute teacher's substitute teacher. At one point, his cellphone went off, betraying a downloaded ring tone that was Mahler's Second Symphony. Meanwhile, a few gibberish-dispensing sycophants, with matching ingratiating smiles and dubious hand-eye coordination, added to the din. They were found circling a certain out-of-town editorialist and all-around bugle-sounder who had the same facility for witty outrage in print as Shakira had with her non-fibbing hips and Heather Mills once did with her gung-ho gold-digging. He, the evening's ostensible star attraction, was tall, blasé, and ginger-maned. The words *think* and *piece* floated daffily from him.

There were lots of people in the room who could justifiably be called "successful," but, as Ravi had deduced over the years of being in rooms much like this, truly successful people were really just the ones who yearned and scraped for it the most. They often oozed medium-grade talent or, if at all, a linear talent. They weren't the best-looking, or the wittiest, or even the most fabulously erudite. They simply had set up fewer distractions for themselves.

Two such alphas stirred beside him as he stood inventorying. "How are you?" "I'm great, how are you?" One stuck out a studious hand; the other went in with an aspirational hug. They improvised with an awkward arm pat, punctuated with post-millennial m-angst. Somewhere in this vicinity, Ravi also heard someone say, with all the spontaneity of a taxidermied butterfly, "History is written by the victors." This, he knew, was old. Quite old. As old as Jennifer Aniston's circa-*Friends* coif and as tired, at least in this particular tribe, as Paris Hilton hawking, "That's hot!" at the MTV Music Awards.

He felt—as he so often did at this sort of hardcover soiree—like suddenly bursting into song. Just to stir things up. Something ABBA, perhaps. That one about Fernando, for instance.

Instead, he multi-tasked by thinking about all the disparate things that swim around in a gossip columnist's head while pretending to be charming at a party: Bikram, Borat, Bugaboo, Deepak, and Barack. Sarkozy and Madoff and Dita Von Teese. Federer, Twitter, Tyra, Feist. Snoop Dogg. André Leon Talley and Hotel du Cap. Posh and Becks. *Jon and Kate Plus 8.* J.J. Abrams and J.K. Rowling. Jonas Brothers and Jimmy Choo. Suri Cruise! Christopher Hitchens. K(C)ates Hudson, Blanchett, and Middleton. Twelvestep, Dsquared^2, Xbox, *Top Chef.*

While at this, of course, he took his puckishness for a sprint through the chintz, whereupon getting a nod from a certain newspaper honcho, he cracked, "It should be an early night. *Project Runway* is on TV tonight, and people are going to start leaving soon to catch it."

Recoiling visibly, the print honcho replied, "They can PVR it."

Uh, yes, Ravi wanted to scream at this obvious culprit of sonorous overseriousness. See that ice on the floor! I just broke it! That's all!

Hoping to fare better, he kept moving, bypassing on his left that TV oracle Rick Mercer, who had managed magically to carve out a scrumptious niche as both a satirist and a suck-up, and on his right, David Frum, a well-bloodlined member of the commentariat most famous for creating the term *axis of evil* for his then-boss, the president of the United States. It was while making his way past a certain brooch-donning battleaxe-about-town that he spotted his final quarry. The hostess of the night; the woman of the manor. Ever the fawn, even in her *sotto voce* seventh decade, Lady Ivory was backed into a corner and looked like she'd rather be shopping for caftans and applying Crème de la Mer.

She was a wisp of a thing with a ghostly pallor and a crisp, crimson line of a mouth. She had written many books but never a grocery list. A famous insomniac, known for her fashionable shrubbery, she had married much, held court, traded up. Though her husband's empire now lay in tatters, and he sat in the legal cesspool where bits of Enron also floated and faced the prospect of the slammer, she remained in devoted Tammy Wynette mode. Ravi, in his way, had no doubt that she did love her husband, in her way. It was even slightly romantic, he was inclined to think. Together, Lord and Lady Ivory cuddled in a tiny tent of daily devotion amid a jeering jungle of envy and hate.

"I brought you this," he butted in, after waiting for the opportune time to interrupt but realizing there was none. He handed the hostess a pack of British wine gums that he'd been keeping safe in his Canali-sponsored herringbone sports jacket. The jacket, he noticed, smelled like last night's party.

"Something to chew on," he mentioned, pointing to the pack.

"Stay right here," hissed the Lady, who used to be known as Kim and once, years and years ago, had worn cut-off jean shorts (he had the incriminating pictures to prove it). Her deep coal-like eyes, circumscribed by deep coal-like mascara, fixed on him for an instant before flicking to someone over his shoulders. "I want to talk to you later."

Whoosh, she was gone. Gone faster than Alex Trebek's moustache. Never to return. Not on this night, anyway. But as she left, he noticed that there was the memory of a scent, in the way that there is with all the great Mistresses of the Universe. Rupert Everett, the actor, had explained it best when extrapolating not long ago on some of the fab bitch-goddesses he'd had the luck to appear with on the silver screen. About Madonna, with whom he did that movie about best friends and yoga and conceiving, and also Julia Roberts, with whom he starred in that movie where, in one scene, all those people in a restaurant erupt into a chorus of "I Say a Little Prayer for You." Rupert had said there was always—always, always, always—the prevailing, trailing consommé of sweat.

"There is a male quality to the female superstar," he'd summed up. One that must be if she is to survive, and so "she becomes a kind of she-man, a beautiful woman with invisible balls," and that inescapable B.O. is a "strange and a powerful reminder, attractive and terrifying, of who is wearing the trousers." It marked her territory. And here it seemed it was the case with Lady Ivory: her excretion had no bounds.

This scene done with, Ravi decided to meander and prowl and poke. Took the opportunity, too, to sample the duck quesadilla—gourmet-expressed from Pusateri's—which, in turn, prompted a pun-happy economist in the room to hit him with the question, "Ravi, do you quesadilla and tell?" Stopped long enough, naturally, to tiny-talk with Jason Doughton, one of the wealthiest of the avidly single, new-generation gents in the country, who, it must be said, always had an appreciative smile to spare for Ravi because, years ago, the latter had run into Doughton deep in the heart of Gaytown, where he was on an obvious date with a woman who looked like a Nubian princess and was distinctly not the young buck's then-society-appropriate girlfriend. Because Ravi had resisted the temptation to write about the incident—meeting your mistress in Gaytown, he did think, was pretty ingenious—and because, moreover, he'd never acknowledged the incident outright to the guy, a wonderful well of goodwill had developed between them. A well of goodwill based on, to put it squarely, the following premise: Jason knew that he owed Ravi, and Ravi knew that Jason knew he owed Ravi, and though Ravi had never made any overtures in this direction, both knew it was just a matter of time before the die was cast.

As a chronicler of people, Ravi knew that not writing about something often gave him more capital than actually writing about it.

Making his way solo into the empty, three-storey oval library, where the babble significantly receded, he saw countless war tomes, historical bios, out-of-date atlases, and a rather well-trampled copy of *The Robber Bride. The Lover* by Marguerite Duras sat next to J.G. Ballard's *Empire of the Sun.* It was an insanely handsome room in a *Gosford Park* sort of way, and not surprisingly, he also saw Lord Ivory's own book, a rather festive diatribe about General George Patton. A copy of it was sitting, as a matter of fact, face down on a drop-leaf desk next to a monstrous gold-plated globe. Underneath, when he snooped, he found, to his extreme astonishment, a copy of *Twilight,* that *sine qua non* teen tale of star-crossed vampire-mortal love.

Before he even had time to gasp at the discovery, however, a man who looked like an orderly, or maybe a good Jesuit, appeared before him. He was needlessly tall. He wore clogs and a sweater vest, and had cheeks even pinker, if it was possible, than the Ralph Lauren dress that Gwyneth Paltrow famously wore when she took her Oscar for *Shakespeare in Love.* He was dripping with disgust—not unlike the look dispensed by most Romans when they see a stupid-o American ordering a cappuccino at dinner. Ravi took a step back and began to say, "How nice to see you," but the man stopped him and leaned in close, very close, to deliver an important message.

"If you write about this party, I'll kill you."

3

"I Just Want to Focus on My Salad"

Ravi didn't usually break a sweat. Not unless he'd eaten some lamb vindaloo first.

Ever since the night of the lower-tax-inclined eggheads, though, he had been just a little nervous. In fact, truth be told, the last time his body coursed with such discomfiture was when Ryan Gosling and Rachel McAdams broke up, thus robbing him and the country of an all-Canuck power-cute-duo to root for.

There was something about the strange, sweater-vested man's voice. He couldn't quite place it.

If you write about this party, I'll kill you. That is what Mr. Sweater Vest had said, unveiling a menacing row of lower teeth—tiny Chiclets of pure evil! Was it a real *Sopranos*-worthy threat or a mere vestige of that well-known Canadian, held-over-from-Great-Britain irony? And, if it was the former, he couldn't, he had to admit, help getting just a little turned on. People always went on and on about how he—Canada's best-known globetrotting, dish-delivering people-watcher—was such a gentlemanly gossip.

So it was nice to hear that someone found him actually threatening, especially since, height-wise, he tended more toward the Michael J. Fox than the Michael Jordan.

He still wrote about the party, complete with the *Twilight* vampire shocker, because no one puts baby in the corner, to quote *Dirty Dancing* (or was that Milan Kundera?). And, besides, do those moody, marble-mouthed people on *CSI* refuse to do their prowling just because of a little suggested danger? The whole thing gave him an enchanted rush.

Even now, sitting some days later on a carpet of beach in Anguilla—yes, another one of those really gruelling journalistic travel junkets—he couldn't help mulling it. Just then, his phone sang.

"Where are you?" rang out the trilling voice of the person who was secretly next of kin.

"A dot in the Caribbean," he said before disgorging more information that nobody who isn't in the Caribbean wants to hear. "In Anguilla. Took the chopper from St. Maarten, the Dutch side. What rhymes with kiss, Rory? It's bliss. Major bliss. They say that St. Barts is the place to go in order to be seen, but that Anguilla is the place to go to disappear. And did I mention that Beyoncé and Jay-Z have come here often?"

"Well, how wonderful for them," Rory tarted and then abruptly stopped. "But, listen, when can I see you? When are you back?"

"Well, I'm on a bit of a world tour," he encapsulated, not exactly lying. "But you know I love you, my sweet kebab."

"What about your column?"

"Oh, Rory. In the immortal words of Chuck Bass on *Gossip*

Girl, 'Don't get your La Perlas in a bunch!' You know my editors never really know where I am. I make my deadlines. I dish, I carve. The readers are amused. And the show, it goes merrily on."

"We need to talk," she said, overpassing him quickly and moving into another conversational lane.

"Rory. We'll talk. I promise you. It's just that Anguilla, as a destination, is really, really, *really* hot right now, and if I don't experience it at this very second, it might be over by sunset. You know how it is with these It Spots . . ."

"Oh, Ravi."

"And y'know, it's important not to Zellweger it when it comes to the important moments in life."

"Reference, please." It was true that Rory sometimes needed a translator when talking to Ravi.

"In other words, my sweetheart, you can't be in the washroom when you they're calling out your name for a Golden Globe. And I can't be talking to you on the telephone when there's a brilliant midday sun situation happening in Anguilla right before my very eyes."

"But have you not heard anything, Ravi? Surely they've decided by now?"

"No word yet, but just as soon we hear, everything will be grand and we can be out!" He paused. "For now, Rory, I just want to focus on my salad."

"Reference again, please," she tried.

"In other words, my sweetheart, I don't want to talk about it. Like Martha Stewart, who kept on chopping her cabbage and said, 'I just want to focus on my salad' when she appeared on

CBS's *The Early Show* one morning, all those years ago, right after the news broke about her stock mess, I'd prefer right now just to focus on my Caribbean hot spot."

Rory drew in a deep, appeasing breath, and then she sassed, "Okay, we'll speak later, you no-good husband, you. And, please, don't do anything I would do."

They exchanged tenderest goodbyes, and after putting the conversation firmly out of his mind, he walked out of that tableau and onto a veranda. Beautiful. The sun was, indeed, up to some excellent hijinks—a swell bit of set decoration on this otherwise yawn of a place where the goats outnumber people and the living is easier than Michael Phelps's butterfly stroke.

Lunch. Yes, he was in the mood for some. All this hot-spot investigating—islands like this depended on gossip columnists to keep the buzz coming—had made him super-hungry.

Seated, soon enough, in an exalted resort hotel called Malliouhana, he looked out onto the enormous bustline of ocean horizon, clinging to the petticoat of white sand. It was the sort of exonerating place that was gung-ho Grecian in design—think Nana Mouskouri in a bathtub full of olive oil—and the cooking, for some unclear reason, *vraiment* French. Pulling out his MacBook Air, making sure to keep one eye on the mangoed sun and one eye on the laptop, he began filing away a few items for his column because while wonders never ceased, neither did his deadlines.

Okay, where was he? Oh yeah, Steve Nash, one of the greats where basketball players were concerned, and certainly the greatest ever to come out of Canada. While Ravi had been beaching it up out of town, the hoop artist had been spotted partying in Toronto, and thanks to a cavalry of spies as well as this really cool thing called the World Wide Web, Ravi hadn't missed a beat.

"I see, I hear," he began typing in his familiar refrain, "that Canada's gift to the NBA, Steve Nash, was out having the best of times at Lobby last Thursday, in a room full of chicks who looked like Lindsay Lohan and men who grew up eating challah bread and now use Axe Body Spray!

"Later—much later," he continued, "Nash set off for a dusky underground bar downtown so compact he kept banging his head on the low-beamed ceiling! And to think, Nash is actually considered one of the shorter basketball players out there! Would Magic Johnson have even gotten through the door?"

"Take that, Gabriel García Márquez!" he muttered to himself.

But then, wondering whether he had overdone it with the exclamation marks and whether he ought to remove some of them—were three too many in one paragraph? maybe downsize to two?—his eyes happened upon the menu that had been dropped off at his table.

After years of doing what he did, Ravi knew a story when he saw one. An exclamation mark or two would go off in his head, complete with actual lines being cranked up on that other keyboard, the one that sat between his ears.

And this story, it just happened to be one that came with anchovies. His attention had been wrested away from basketball to greens when he noticed that the Caesar salad was no mere Caesar. More specifically, it read, the Michel Rostang Caesar salad.

Rostang, he knew, was a Michelin-starred chef from Paris. Part of the fifth generation of a distinguished French cooking family, he was as much of a household name there as the Seine. Having not had much luck spotting any actual stars of screen or song here so far—a few bad days on the market for a social columnist—Ravi knew he finally had something that could work in the column! There was a boldface possibility, and boldfaces, after all, were the be-all, the end-all, the bottom line.

Years ago now, he quickly learned from the server, the chef had skipped off to Anguilla, having developed an idler's taste for the island. Nowadays, he acted as the chief consultant for this particular hotel's food-stop.

Which brings us to the salad. Many a bed of greens had Ravi seen before, but never had he come across a canopy of this precise nature, where a chef was willing to attach his very name to it. In the spirit of Martha Stewart, he thought he would turn his focus to it.

"What makes a Michel Rostang Caesar salad different from any old Caesar?" he asked the server, who was, thankfully, on island time and more than open to all and any inquiries. "It's his specialty," came the answer. After which he was told that, in addition to Rostang's top-secret dressing, it came with a precious poached egg on top.

"You can have it without the egg if you want. Many people do," said the peon with the pad.

"No, no," Ravi exclaimed. "If I'm going to have it, I'm going all the way."

And so he ordered. And waited. And frothed in his head: Are

eponymous salads the new next thing? Surely, why not? Since easy-on-the-ego chefs already name fine restaurants after themselves—Jean Georges in New York, Vij's in Vancouver, Nobu everywhere—wasn't this the next logical step? To name-game with a dish? Put one's moniker on a monkfish? Stake one's rep on an actual steak!

After Ravi spent much time staring out into the calms of the British West Indies, the salad finally transpired. The firm poached egg was spread out like a ballerina in *The Nutcracker.* The leaves beneath it were chic and slightly pouf, their silhouette akin to something out of Dior's renowned New Look from the 1950s.

Ravi's verdict? More than pretty good. He made a sound usually associated with lovemaking.

"He mixes the anchovies into the dressings," Ravi was later told by the increasingly avuncular server. "It's good, no?" Mister, he wanted to reply, if one is on assignment and one can't have a live celebrity—say, a Ben Affleck or a Jennifer Garner—a celebrity salad will do the trick.

Or does it?

Later that afternoon, an overanxious island guide with a perm—and that perennial look of someone with too much sand in her pants—took Ravi over to one of Anguilla's great modern monuments. It was where Jen and Brad effectively had their last low-cal, high-protein supper.

During Christmas 2004—as everyone who knows their *US Weekly* knows—the requiem began for Aniston and Pitt's relationship when they landed in these warmest of climes. Just days after the trip, the then-Hollywood Sweethearts announced their shocking split to the universe.

Ravi and the overanxious tour guide rode to the side of the island where lay a villa called Altamer. Outside, the ocean was calm; waves lapped gently at the shoreline, making a soft shushing sound. Smashing by any definition, and a mere US$75,000 a week, the building itself was a massive, white-on-white beachfront house designed to look like the world's most expensive toilet roll. Needless to say, an entire chorus line of on-call servants came along with the digs.

While there, Ravi even got to see the master suite. The bed—so big it had been lifted on a crane and carried through the upper balcony doors, he was told—came smooshed with an astounding thirteen pillows. Yes, he counted. And, while doing so, he lamented that the bed had hardly any room for humans. No wonder it didn't work out between Jen and Brad, he surmised to himself.

Though being on the celebrity beat, day after day, sunset after sunset, was supposed to have made Ravi hardened, suspicious, and, well, jaded as hell, it, curiously, had wreaked the opposite effect on him. In his case, he was more emphatic now than he had been only a few short years ago. Was it because he knew, more than many perhaps, what a mural most people's lives were, how quick so many were to draw up caricatures of each other, and how easily a life could be distilled down to one scene, one comment, one quirk, instead of that scene or comment or quirk being but just one brush stroke in the wider picture? Yes. Yes. He knew this because he did plenty of that brush-stroking himself in his day/night job. And, so, in a weird way, doing the social beat had forced him to flick off the harness of his own preconceptions. And covering celebrities? Strangely—and this was sometimes hard to explain—it had actually made him more sensitive to real people. Whatever, of course, "real" meant.

At this juncture, he took the opportunity to hold a little Hollywood vigil amid the thirteen pillows, and a part of him half-seriously mourned.

4

Parties, Porta-Potties, and Hyberbole

Finished with the salad beat, Ravi refocused his energies on fast fashion.

Expected in Los Angeles a few days later for an H&M party, of all things, he barrelled his way across the skies. In one of the airports during one of the stops between one of the connections, where our intrepid reporter sat in repose trying to affect his Bill Murray-in-*Lost-in-Translation* look, and as a Muzak version of "The First Cut Is the Deepest" wafted up from a craptastic sound system, he wondered what it would be like to have a private plane. He'd been on a few in his time, but what would it be like to have on-call wings in the manner of that lucky lady who'd married that famous son of a Canadian legacy, the one whose surname you could hardly get through the day without seeing at least once. This particular broad, it was said, had recently flown to Paris Fashion Week, not only on her own jet, but with her own hairdresser and around-the-clock makeup artist! Lost in his reverie, Ravi noticed another broad, a gnarled woman in a Juicy Couture suit, making airport eyes at him.

Tucking in his stomach just a tad, he readied himself to say, "Thank you so much" to the woman, who was obviously from Canada, and who was obviously gearing herself up to tell Ravi that she just loved his column, never missed his weekly appearances on morning television, had framed that glowing profile of him recently in *Celsius* magazine, and thought he was, gee, the greatest thing since Crocs.

After several minutes of prolonged I-know-you-from-somewhere staring, she opened her mouth and let it hang for a bit, just like Dame Kiri Te Kanawa probably does right before doing scales. And then the woman blurted out, "I just loved your movie!"

"Excuse me, *Ms.*?"

"The sequel was just okay, but the original, it was dope."

He gave her a quizzical once-over.

"Kumar, right? I'm so sorry, I dunno know your real name."

Okay, then. This woman in Juicy thought he was that dude in the stoner comedy *Harold & Kumar Go to White Castle* who unexpectedly had gone on to work in the Obama administration. Next thought: time maybe to check in with the office. Grabbing his cell, while conceding an I'm-busy smile to the woman opposite, Ravi dialled the digits for his editor, Sam. He was an atrium of a man who was always good at condemnation and liked all the palace-intrigue stuff almost as much as Ravi did.

"Anything I should know?" he posed, pacing, when Sam's voice came banging through.

"Ravi! How's my favourite wanker doing? I was just gonna call you," the editor husked.

He knew better than to ask where Ravi was geo-wise, so instead just carried on. "So, d'ya think you're mentioning this Daisy Emerson person too much? She's just a publicist, dammit."

"A publicist who does a very good job of publicizing, I'll have you know. Herself, primarily," Ravi defended. "She regularly calls in with her own sightings, and it's not like I don't occasionally need the material. Last week she called me to tell me she'd been at Le Petit Castor, where she had the arugula salad and a nice Shiraz. I find it all vaguely amusing."

"Okay, whatever," said Sam, satisfied somewhat. "Tell me: how's that item on Belinda Stronach comin' along?"

Sam was referring to the infamous Canadian heiress-turned-politician-turned-ex-politician who was a virtual kleptomaniac when it came to newspaper headlines. Being a woman with power and money who also had a rich and readable love life—and had not long ago conquered cancer—she had been, over the many years, like a Tiffany-wrapped gift box to the nation's media. When he'd run into her more recently at a party, she'd told him that she'd taken up both "vegan" and "yoga" following her health scare, and, no, she informed Ravi, when he'd had the temerity to ask, she "did not miss steak frites." Quote-unquote. But this was not what Sam was referring to.

"I'm still working on it," the expert people-watcher said, not exactly lying.

"Okay, 'cause it's a good story . . . and, hey, Rav, who the fuck is this Mr. Darcy? Sounds pretty gay. He called a few hours ago and left a message saying he's looking for you. I'm not sure why he didn't just call you on your line . . ."

"Mr. Darcy?"

"Yeah."

"As in, the object of affection from *Pride and Prejudice*? As in, Jane Austen?"

"Or that big, fat, freakin' rip-off *Bridget Jones.* Christ, Helen Fielding made a shitload of money . . ."

Suddenly, there in the limboland between flights, Ravi lapsed into a complex silence. Then, "Wait, what did this Mr. Darcy say? What exactly did he say?" He considered the possibility that he sounded just a wee bit frantic.

"Shit all. He was returning your call, I thought . . . Wait, Rav, is something wrong?"

"No. Yes. I don't know."

"Do you or do you not know this Mr. Darcy?"

"I know a man in a sweater vest."

"What the . . . ?"

"And clogs. He was wearing clogs!"

"Ravi, uh . . . have you been watching *Lost* again?"

"When was this?" he persisted.

But he didn't get the answer nor did he get a chance to ask any more questions because somebody at a gate was calling his name, and this gate wasn't at all pearly. Ravi's flight to L.A. was itching to leave the tarmac.

"Yikes, I have to get on a plane . . . I'll call you later, Sam."

Mr. Darcy, Mr. Darcy, Mr. Darcy. He repeated the suddenly dangerous mantra all the way into the just-in-the-nick-of-time jet. He was having that sickly hunch again. Luckily, though (because Ravi was the kind of guy who depended on the kindness of sponsors), he was flying first class today, and with all the paranoia he was carrying around he really could use all the legroom he could get.

Clearly, the demonic man he'd run into in the library inside Lord and Lady Ivory's house last week was trying to send him a message. But what? And why? And what now?

Anxious at this point, but also spent by the suspicion, Ravi reclined his chair and tried to find solace in a siesta. Sleep being the perfect antidote to an afternoon of jet-setting and the M. Night Shyamalan–style creeps, it wasn't long before he'd acquiesced to it.

Many winks later, he was firmly in the clutches of La-La Land. Not much after that, he was tenderized in lotion and swimming in the pool at the fabulous Bel-Air Hotel. It was one of those classic L.A. days that feels like the spiritual equivalent to an all–Veuve Clicquot lunch on an empty stomach.

Care- and worry-free all of a sudden—L.A. does have that effect—he took in the sun and the breeze and tried to think nice thoughts. He thought about Farrah Fawcett, young and unrenovated and still married to the Six Million Dollar Man. He thought of Faye Dunaway when she was still relatively sane and could rock a beret like nobody else. He thought of Beach Boys serenades.

The Bel-Air was one of Ravi's favourite spots in the whole wide world and hardly the sort of non-hoi-polloi place he could afford if he, heaven forbid, ever actually paid for hotels. (Gosh, what would that be like?) The hotel was like a soundstage, a famously manicured L.A. hideaway that came with privilege, privacy, and its own swan lake. Liz Taylor had at least one of her weddings here; come to think of it, so had that singularly saga-sagged Britney Spears.

But how time flies when you're doing laps and a gang of tanorexics—the kind quite specific to L.A.—hold mirth on a bunch of pool chairs right beside you. Getting out of the pool, he noticed that the "Samantha" in this foursome had with her the teeniest Birkin bag he'd ever seen, right there by the pool, to go along, presumably, with the teeniest two-piece she was working. Eyeing the total package, he remembered what the daughter of the woman who was the namesake of the almighty arm-candy, singer Jane Birkin, had once said about the name bag to an interviewer. The daughter, French pinup Charlotte Gainsbourg, when asked in an interview if she herself carried the Hermès in question, had replied plainly and with one of those unqualified Gallic duhs, "No way. Would you carry a handbag named after your mother?"

Towelling off, he inadvertently splashed some drops on the miniature Birkin, which earned him quite a death stare from its owner—one probably not seen since the Romanians finally did in that Ceauşescu dictator guy. No time like the present to make a getaway—for more reason than one! Ravi was, indeed, on the cusp of being late for the very H&M fashion bash he'd travelled all this way to attend and dispatch about. Cleansing and changing quickly into his oft-party uniform of jeans/blazer/skinny tie, he power-spritzed himself with some Penhaligon's Blenheim, topped his metaphoric fedora, and left the building. If there was one thing he knew how to do in a jiff, it was to get ready for an evening out.

The party, in a Bel Air bungalow some palm trees away, was in full, glorious swing when he arrived. Wow, he said to himself, allowing as many exclamation points as he could manage. Triple wow. You ain't in Kamloops anymore, Ravi.

A word, now, on the state of the H&M party in the modern age: some time after the start of the last millennium, someone, somewhere, decreed that the buzziest fashion rested on the Swedish shoulders of this cheapest-of-cheap-chic retailers. After spreading through the world like a nineteenth-century colonial power, and having the likes of the Material Girl pose in their ads, and then unburdening a series of brilliantly limited high-low collaborations with the likes of Stella McCartney and Roberto Cavalli, the clothier threw parties that endeared themselves to even the most jaded clothes-monger.

Ravi, no novice to this gravy train, once also travelled seventeen hours to attend the launch of H&M in China, of all places. That party, he recalled, was held at the Shanghai Science and

Technology Museum, which really did befit the comic-book spires of that 22-million-people-deep megalopolis. As part of the festivities, the diminutive down-under Kylie Minogue had been recruited, no joke, to help usher in the Swedish takeover of the Middle Kingdom. And to help set the scene, at the entrance were four hundred cute underage girls, all lined up in row after row on steps outside the museum. They were all, amazingly, the same height, and they all sported the same pigtails, and all of them rocked the same silver tracksuits. And they sang. Oh did they sing, sweet voices making tremendous use of the Kylie songbook. It came out, more or less, as phonetic, lending the girl choir an overmedicated, *Invasion of the Chinese Body Snatchers* feel and giving the whole scene the texture of one of those Cultural Revolution rallies, although everybody was quite sure that the *M* in H&M did not stand for Mao. By the time the actual Disco Queen came on inside, she warbled for about fifteen minutes—or, to put it another way, for .01470588 percent of the full seventeen hours it had taken Ravi to get to China. Naturally, it had been worth every second. His point being: this cheap and cheerful retailer really did put out when they were throwing a party. And not only had they become famous for their over-the-topness, but, more poignantly, they had left the old-school fashion houses of Paris and Milan looking just a touch dusty. A sign of the times, one might say. Democracy at work, one was also tempted to add.

"Don't it just make you believe in fuckin' love all over again?" asked one of the other journos he was now rolling with.

Potty-mouthed Pollyanna had a point, he did have to admit.

This particular party, done up like the wedding of the century, was a celebration of the marriage between H&M and that totally droll Dutch designing duo Viktor & Rolf. While a shifting melee of paparazzi lunged and snapped, the evening's star fashion-designer extraterrestrials—spectacled and dressed identically, as per usual—stood in a gazebo with the glamazonic model of the nano-second. It was both a threesome and a traditional receiving line.

"Care for a mojo-ito?" asked a woman dressed up as a geeky bridesmaid. She was holding up a tray that presumably bore the night's signature drink. On each of the individual glasses *You Go Groom!* was etched in gold.

"No thanks," said Ravi. Proceeding to make the rounds, he began to compile his party checklist.

Check: the ferocious flurry of flowers placed everywhere in the gigantic back garden—all of them scientifically engineered to be taller and whiter than anything you'd find in nature.

Check: the full, black-tied orchestra, on hand to unleash campy classical takes on George Michael's "Careless Whisper," "Billie Jean" à la Michael Jackson, and, most affecting, a percussion-heavy nod to "The Girl from Ipanema."

Check: the Tinseltown-appropriate guests for what was a traditional Hollywood wedding, including such cats as Mario Lopez, Chloë Sevigny, Kanye West, Chow Yun-Fat, Zachary Quinto, a few of the kids from *The Hills,* one ex-Bachelor with cobblestone abs, and two whole Olsen Twins. (Also kicking around was at least one next of kin of the former Shah of Iran, because, well, honestly . . . does a turtleneck really fall in the forest of fashion if a deposed royal isn't there to see it?)

Check, check, check: the peals of bells, the flutes of bubbly, the simulated horse-carriage sounds, a bouquet waiting to be tossed at the end of the fashion show!

"Simply beyond!" That was what the *Daily Telegraph*'s ubiquitous Hilary Alexander was extolling when Ravi happened upon a circle of à la mode insiders. "I've never seen anything like it," was the hyperbolic kudos coming from another long-time stalwart, *Fashion Television* queen Jeanne Beker. Two thumbs-up, she mimed. Nearby, in yet another fashion flock, huddled that front-row fixture Ingrid Sischy, who never failed to look like some fabulous version of your grade ten driving instructor; that Suzy Menkes, from the *International Herald Tribune*, who always made the scene in her signature sausage-roll bun; and that other guy, from *Vogue*, with the old-fashioned man-bob, who always gave good *Remains of the Day.*

Having seen these same people at shows in New York, Milan, and Paris, Ravi considered how nice it was to have them to look at while waiting for shows to crank up. Not to mention comforting. Somehow, it added to the ritual of these fashion affairs and simultaneously drove home the precise clubbiness of the whole enterprise. Looking at all the familiar faces, he was struck by how tight the international circle in fashion—even H&M fashion—truly was. It made admission to the European Union look facile in comparison.

It also struck him how each tribe had its own vivid machinations and hierarchies, gossip and unspoken rules, and, being someone who moved between tribes—and what was he if not a tribe-traveller?—Ravi knew it was the same-old same-go in almost every circle. Whether it was a fashion show or an art event, a book thing or a music shindig, or even a party packed tight with politicos.

Except, perhaps, for the fact that the fashion world did, indeed, take the Magnolia Bakery cupcake when it came to late starts. So, a word now on the state of waiting at fashion shows in the current epoch: in a way, waiting was part of the show, and waiting was all there was. And though the cooling of heels at these shows was anything but rare, the tardy designer phenom reached its most dizzying apex a few years ago in Manhattan when Marc Jacobs got his show going at the un-neat hour of 11 p.m.—nearly two hours after its appointed time. This unleashed a torrent of complaints and lots of pent-up fashionista frustration, led fearlessly by the aforementioned sausage-roll-bunned reporter from the *Tribune,* who wrote a ghastly review of the show and said of the boy-wonder designer, "I would like to murder him with bare hands and never see another Marc Jacobs show in my entire life." After some passage of time, of course, everyone calmed right down, and Suzy and Marc too ostentatiously made up, but not before some more trading of insults, and rumours even surfaced on the web that the designer had actually been spotted at the bar at the Mercer Hotel in Soho on the night in question at about 9:30, long after guests had taken their seats at his runway. Naturally, this prompted some of Jacobs's supporters to unveil photographic evidence showing that Marc was, in fact, backstage at the alleged time.

It had been said before and it would be said again, but fashion really was murder. And with the orchestra now getting going on a jazzy wedding march, it seemed to Ravi that it was assassination time once again here in Los Angeles. He turned, upped his gaze.

So, yeah, the clothes. Loopy, yes. Lovely too. When the models—all of them young and malleable—appeared on the catwalk, it was obvious that Viktor & Rolf had managed to incorporate both a sense of play and nifty detailing into the collection. The sum total, running the male-female gamut, included standards such as the trench, the white shirt, pyjamas—pyjamas!—and the little black dress. Not to mention a not-so-little wedding dress!

Ravi was at that point standing on top of a chair in a moodily lit area with a recently separated (and now water-retaining) actress who'd seen better days, weeks, and hours. Watching him watching her, he noticed, was a fellow tribesman—a gossipist who toiled in New York.

"Fancy meeting you here," said Ravi, coming down from his perch to greet the fellow, who was tall and taciturn and whose parents had fled Lithuania from the Soviets so that their child would one day grow up to, ostensibly, report on Kim Kardashian's booty. Though they had their respective domains, Ravi had a familial thing going with most of his fellow pro-snoopers. It was a small circle. And celebrity being as porous as it is these days, national borders didn't make an ounce of diff.

"I read your item about Colin Farrell," this fellow pro-snooper began to say. (In the world of organized gossip, columnists always referred to stories as "items." It was the inside-baseball giveaway!)

"Oh, yeah?" Ravi rang back.

"I was wondering," the other guy went on, beading his eyes just so, "when you said you saw Colin Farrell walking arm in arm with that girl, was that arm-link in the style where two people might just be cold and hover together or was it like an *arm-link* arm-link?"

Ravi thought for a second, smiled a big one. "The former, I would say."

Standing there, the tattle and the tattle, it occurred to both of them that gossip, as it had been said, was like standing on a roof on a windy day shredding a feather pillow and then trying to collect the feathers later.

Having clearly imbibed too much gratis bubbly at this point, Ravi decided it was time to make a visit to the loo. On the way—as all the beautiful and bronzed were just starting to do the sway that comes before the dance—he crossed the path of Warren Beatty, who was hanging off every word that Annette Bening, the woman who tamed him, was saying. Like a well-trained husband. Odd to think he'd gone from *Bonnie & Clyde* to H&M. The company must have promised their four children a lifetime supply of school clothes—or something. But it was just then that Ravi ran into Viktor. Or, gosh, was it Rolf? Being of the opinion that it's never too late to pump for a freshly squeezed quote, he cornered the peculiar designer and asked, "Hey, did you guys sign a pre-nup before you got married to H&M?"

The one-half of the Dutch duo gave a genuine-article cackle. Then he said, "No, because we always knew there was going to be a divorce."

Ravi transmitted a you're-a-genius grin and then fled just as soon as he could. He really did have to go. On the way to the loo, which was actually a porta-potty in the bushes, but the most beautifully lacquered porta-potty he'd ever seen (because, well, this was just the kind of party it was, and Los Angeles really was known to have the most beautiful porta-potties in the world), he shuddered to find that someone was already lurking behind the door he'd flung open.

It was the alleged Mr. Darcy.

"I've been waiting for you," he murmured, sounding like a constipated Hannibal Lecter.

The clogs were the same, but the sweater vest was de rigueur Viktor & Rolf. It took Ravi a few seconds to come up with an appropriate bon mot.

"I have no money," he finally managed. "I'm a journalist."

"Don't be ridiculous!" the menace in the porta-potty exclaimed. "And don't be scared! I want your help . . . with, uh, a little situation."

Ravi's turn: "Can we possibly talk about it somewhere else. Say, Katsuya? Tomorrow at noon? Or maybe Hyde tomorrow night? Come to think of it, I've always wanted to dine at Cut, where Tom and Katie had their engagement party. But, of course, we can do Spago if you're more old school."

"It's not safe here," came the reply.

He clarified that by "here," he meant all of Los Angeles. He further explained that he was an old friend of Lady Ivory, which is why he'd been at her house the other night, and that he ran some sort of "boutique operation" out of L.A. It had been suggested to him that Ravi had the "qualities" to help with a "celebrity client situation" up in Canada.

"But what? And why me? And how'd you know you'd find me

at an H&M party, of all places?" beseeched Ravi, his sentences running into each other.

"I have my ways," arrived the answer right out of Cliché Scriptwriting 101. "We tête-à-tête back in Toronto," he ordered next with staccato precision. "Tuesday. Next week. The Spoke Club. On King Street. One p.m. I never do noon lunches, okay? Never."

Ravi nodded. What else was he going to do? "So you're not going to kill me?" he quickly thought to ask next.

"No, I'm not going to kill you," Mr. Darcy baby-talked back. "Why would you think that?"

"Well, you did, um, kind of threaten me in the library at Lady Ivory's party," Ravi reminded. Somewhere in the distance, outside the porta-potty, Morrissey's whining nasal was coming at them from the DJ booth. He was singing about going out tonight but not having a stitch to wear.

"Oh, Ravi. I thought you, of all people, would appreciate a little drawing-room irony. No need to take everything so literally."

"Yes, sir."

"Any more questions?" hailed the alleged Mr. Darcy, pretty disingenuously, come to think of it.

Ravi nodded yet again. "Just one thing. Can I go now?"

5

Vile Bodies

Last year, cross his heart and hope to die, Ravi overheard someone say something to someone that he's, well, never managed to forget. It was in the bellows of a subterranean bar in Toronto known as And/Or, renowned, in no particular order, for its steep drinks, fancy-pants, and proprietor with well-attended-to torso.

"I'm from Sudan," is how he remembers the conversation commencing from one side.

The next part of the exchange is what really brought on the chills. "Really?" boomed the somebody else, who was just shy of being a fashion plate and more like a fashion saucer. "I've so always wanted to go to that festival!"

"Festival?" posed the poor, confused Sudanese.

Nobody had the strength or the time to continue with the *Three's Company/Curb Your Enthusiasm* banter any further, so the conversation concluded pretty much there, and Ravi went right back to eyeballing the two clumps of people one could always count on finding at And/Or: a) young-looking older women with starter marriages and b) gay-looking (mostly) straight men.

But two things did strike the insatiable eavesdropper at this point. First, of course, it was amusing that the one woman had difficulty distinguishing between Sudan, the horribly impoverished, war-torn African nation, and Sundance, the indie-film-fest dream that Robert Redford built among all the piney treetops. Hey, it happens, he thought to himself, trying to be charitable.

But secondly, and more worrying still, the woman actually thought it was possible to be "from Sundance" and didn't realize that Park City, Utah, the town, is where Sundance, the festival, takes place annually and where Ravi found himself most Januarys. This made the gal not just geographically obtuse but also deeply (and perhaps more dangerously) pop culturally confused!

After that night at And/Or, Ravi, who liked to think of himself as a "closet intellectual" (but perhaps that was a stretch too), vowed he'd never be the sort of person who confuses Sudan with Sundance. He even sometimes did a kind of Scientologistic chant to himself when he felt a case of the stupids was about to come on: "I will never be the sort of person who confuses Sudan with Sundance. Never! Never! Never!"

It took a certain commitment not to be stupid. This, Ravi believed. Like the days and months it took him to finally and successfully wean himself off the use of the word *cheers* when signing off on emails. Though a lot of non-Brits were guilty of it (it was a horrible, infectious tic of the present century), he wasn't sure when exactly he'd begun, and it wasn't until Rory pointed out the insanity of it all that he'd relented. "Who do you think you are? Clive Owen? Lily Allen? Sir Richard Attenborough?" Rory one day tsk-tsked. "You don't dare use that tiresome word *cheers* if you're not British!" Realizing she was right—wives usually were—he'd begun the process of deprogramming himself. Fast.

But that was the thing: Ravi was willing to put in the effort to keep stupidity at bay; he was willing to change.

It was just one of the things that the newsman believed in, and on this particular morning, on the precipice of his scheduled lunch with Mr. Darcy, he did a general inventory of what he held to be (mostly) true.

Back in the downtown apartment he rarely ever saw—where he kept a punching bag he sometimes used, and where the oven served as extra storage for gift bags—Ravi considered some other things he strongly believed in. Sitting down on a couch near his indoor garden of gift bags—goodness, he'd been meaning to put this latest crop in the oven—he devised a list.

He believed that lighting was fifty percent of everything.

He believed in telling people only as much as they were prepared to believe.

He believed that the truth was almost always stranger than the tabloids.

He believed in the restorative power of baths.

He believed in true love, if only because the very fact that Danny DeVito and Rhea Perlman had found each other in this life really did mean that there was a lid for every proverbial pot.

He believed that blueberries were an excellent source of antioxidants and that chopsticks, infinitely, made life more of a hoot.

He believed that the people who talk about "keeping it real" are typically the last people who do and are to be generally avoided.

He believed that people with money were not particularly brighter or that much more beautiful, but that money did help those people to hide their flaws, and so money was never something to be underestimated.

He believed in skipping all and any parties on New Year's Eve—except for that one sensational calendar-change night in Kuala Lumpur (not that he was old enough or recovered sufficiently to speak yet of it).

He believed that you can tell a lot about someone from how they dance, and even more from how they karaoke.

And, now, he had one more thing he wanted to add to the great blackboard of believing in his head: he believed that it is probably best to hold it in if you happen to be at a party put on by Swedes at a Los Angeles bungalow.

Alas, on Tuesday, just shy of 1 p.m., just as arranged, Ravi found himself in an elevator being snailed up to the Spoke Club, a membership-only *boite* for trustafarians, corporate players, and black belts in hipsterism. He tried to lull himself into a sense of krishnamurti—that South Asian ritual through which one is totally cleansed of thought—but the prospect of plunging to his death in the elevator got the better of him.

He couldn't help it. Every time he got into the plain, old lift, which had been replaced a couple of times but always came back as plain and as old as before, and which seemed to move slower than the traffic to Muskoka cottage country on the Friday of a long weekend, he thought about the time some years ago when a group of Elite models got stuck. Their agency had been throwing a party at the club, and the elevator literally stopped clicking. What happened, in effect, was that a whole bunch of genetic lottery winners were trapped in the tiny metal cage and proceeded to get very, very stressed out.

"I had models in the elevator calling other models who were inside the party," explained the proprietor of the agency when she'd called the next day to spill on the pandemonium. Which, of course, he wrote up lickety-split because he was canny enough to know that when you have the words *models* and *elevator* in the same sentence, you write as fast as you can.

"A stick-person apocalypse" is what he remembers calling the incident, it also giving him the opportunity to work the terms "assorted Alfies," "manicured man-eaters," and "side fire escape" into his column.

What happened next is that the people behind the King Street club—at that point only a few months old—blew a collective gasket and sent word to him by express mail that he was now formally banned from the place. Rarely had Ravi been prouder. Time doing what it does, however, it wasn't long before all was forgiven, and not long after that those very people at the club started sending him little tidbits to tell him, say, "Shania Twain seen here at the Rooftop at noon. Has a post-divorce glow. Still got great legs."

If there was one thing he'd learned writing a gossip column, Ravi thought, standing in his Pierre Hardy desert boots in this extremely leisurely moving box, it was this: most people's memories were shorter than this elevator ride! Truly. The people who were mad at you one day would not be a week or month from now—they'd even forget why they ever were—and the people who claim to be your best friend today could, and probably would, radically shift allegiances tomorrow. You just had to block out the noise and stick with it. Or as Cher once put it: If it's not going to matter in five years, it don't matter. It was an unbeatable lesson—in both columnizing and in life.

"Ravi-oli!" shrilled a voice when the elevator finally opened and he made his debut.

The woman attached to the voice had long blonde hair—so blonde it was almost white. She had on heels, Christian Louboutin it was obvious, with a brave, six-inch spike, and was sheathed in an expensive mimosa-coloured dress that was a testament, probably, to a strict sit-up regime. Incongruously, she also exuded an overall sex-in-the-back-of-a-Bentley-with-a-bucket-of-Cristal play ethic.

He had seen her around before but had no memory of her name. She, on the other hand, seemingly knew him so well she even had a way-cute nickname for him.

"You're my favourite person—except for my husband," the peroxide provocateur went on. "I thought it was so fun how you talked about that restaurant opening in your little article. It's so true—every restaurant opening I've been to, there's no food! I mean, it's like watching *American Idol* and Simon Cowell not giving us at least one eye roll. I mean, what gives?

"Oh, you're so fun, Ravi-oli!" She wasn't stopping anytime soon. "We should really have lunch again soon!"

To the best of his knowledge, Ravi had never had lunch with this woman whose name he didn't recall. But in the way that people say to one another at parties all the time but never really mean, he responded, "We really should do lunch. It's been too long."

Sliding past him and into the elevator, she nodded, and winking furiously, she said, "Oh and I have a really handsome brother you really need to meet." Then, one last parting shrill, accompanied by what sounded like a raven's caw: "Okey-dokey, Ravi-oli, I'll be in touch!"

Once he'd signed in, and left word that a certain Mr. Darcy would be joining him, our journalist walked into the sitting room of the club. It, like much of the three-floor space, had been done up in consoling waves of cream, butterscotch, almond, pecan, mocha, honey, and tan. The overall look? What, he figured, the office of Manhattan's very finest society gynecologist looked like.

A bout of head-turning hit him as he entered the dining area and was seated, as requested, in a corner. There, in the back, was Jim Balsillie, one of the co-founders of the BlackBerry—an invention that lent Canada as many bragging rights in the twenty-first century as insulin, also discovered in this town, had in another. Two tables down was Elmer Olsen, who'd famously discovered hometown beauty Daria Werbowy, currently one of the models making the biggest bank. He was dining with an older woman who gave off the scent of the burbs—the mom, perhaps, of an underage extraterrestrial beauty he'd run into in the aisles of a 7-Eleven or Canadian Tire?

Having a meeting of his own two tables down from him was the fortuitously named real estate broker Joe Cobra, who'd managed to leverage his non-hissy surname, as well as his tough-guy shell, into a rep as an über-famous condo hawker. The barrage of pound-pound-pound publicity certainly hadn't hurt the cause. (Sample billboard headline, which usually featured Joe's face coming out of a badass snake: "Don't Worry. We Do Bite.")

Two boldface politicians—one snowy-haired, one not—were also at the Spoke this afternoon, sitting tentatively across from each other at yet another table. Theirs was one of the great bromances, and their story had been told many times: boy meets boy, boy's father has fierce rivalry with the other boy's dad, boy and boy become roommates at university (in a place over a shoe store), one boy turns into one of the world's great writers/wonks while the other boy starts his ascent in local politics, the other boy returns to Canada where he begins his own squeeze into politics, both boys duke it out for the leadership of a big political party, the other boy (the newbie to politics) eventually triumphs while the first boy concedes that it is best to keep his friends close and his frenemies even closer. Looking at them now, Ravi thought the whole saga spoke to the very incestuousness—and, well, smallness of the country (and probably most countries)—that men who used to share dish detergent ended up debating each other for the nation's top job. Ravi recalled that he'd once blithely referred to the snowy-haired one in his column as a "lychee martini socialist."

Facing south was an MTV VJ, said to be not so shabby in the saddle, even though he was said to have "wildly unkempt" nether regions, according to a source. Tucked in a booth far away? That city-dwelling director David Cronenberg, upon whose face sat a coolly calibrated pout, halfway between *Dead Ringers* ghoulish and that of someone who's just lost his luggage at Heathrow.

Offering a nod from the other side of the dining room was that thoroughbred-in-a-jersey-dress known as Alexandra Weston. Married to the bed-headed son of the second-richest man in Canada—the Westons owned department stores on both sides of the pond and, among other things, owned a famous grocery chain—she was the Carolyn Bessette Kennedy of, if not the country, at least the Spoke. Her husband, the small-screen star Galen Weston Jr., had co-founded the joint, together with his sibling, Alannah. She, the older sis, made her base in London, was a charmer in the art world, and had, not so long ago, wed wondrously in the English countryside, where the wedding roundup included a play-within-in-a-play scene from *A Midsummer Night's Dream.* With a "particularly memorable Bottom" went the word.

As far as this town went, the Westons were old money, but in the fuller context of these things, Ravi wasn't bold enough to make a definitive demarcation. How old did old money have to be to be really old? And how quickly did new dough take on an autumnal glow? He recalled that even John D. Rockefeller, the very personification of American philanthropy, the one who was as big as big bucks came, was born the child of a work-averse salesman whose father once lay accused of both horse-stealing and sexual peccadilloes. Sometimes all it took was one generation to cast the spell of old on money.

Now, he noticed that Alexandra, a natural beauty in the Vanderbilt/Noxzema mould, was into her quiche almost as much as she was into her handheld device—a matter that surely pleased Mr. BlackBerry just across the way.

Ravi waved at some of the people in the room and pretended not to see the others. Before you knew it, however, the sweater-vested man of his nightmares had appeared before him.

"You're on time?" he said.

"And you're not."

Their server had barely put down a breadbasket when Mr. Darcy, making nice dents into an olive roll, began thunder-bolting off both their orders.

"You're having the beef," Mr. Darcy declared.

"Speaking of which," Ravi thought it was only right to say then, "where is it?"

Mr. Darcy, who today had on a vest that was shamrock green, leaned in and in gravelly Christopher Walken tones gave him the take-it-or-leave-it drill. There was a not-so-famous young actress who needed a timeout. She was going to be sent to Canada because it was felt by her minders that Los Angeles was a bad influence on her and so was, for that matter, all of the United States of America. She needed a local minder and some polishing in order to get limelight-ready. Ravi, it was thought, would be the perfect candidate.

"But who are you?" Ravi managed to spit out.

"I'm one of those operatives that deals with extra-exclusive clients," said the man, further attacking the breadbasket like it was Kandahar. Ravi noticed he said the word *exclusive* with a lot of oomph, and that he appeared to have at least some semblance of a rich interior life.

Mr. Darcy then took a moment to pull a disk out of his man-purse and grunted. “See for yourself. You’ll note my past work, references, etc. Feel free to keep this, by the way.”

“But why me?” Ravi tried to rebut. “I only write about celebrities, and sometimes even make fun of them. I’m no Mary Poppins. Nor am I Henry Higgins.”

“Listen, kid. Do you like Old Hollywood? Dream of a time when stars were really stars and journos really had power? That *Sweet Smell of Success* stuff?”

“You could say that.”

“Well, this is your chance. You’re a nice writer. You have a way with words. People seem to like you and believe you. At least some of the time. But this is brass-ring time. Like in those Old Hollywood days . . .”

Mr. Darcy stopped to sneeze—an effect that came out pretty girly and, juxtaposed with his old-man jowls, made him, in Ravi’s mind, just an itsy bit more endearing. Inspecting his face, Ravi noticed that his lunching seatmate had missed a spot while shaving.

“Like those Old Hollywood days when the studios and agents worked hand in hand with the press, you know?” Mr. Darcy continued. “What you’re going to do is be a friend to this actress. Not much else. Guide her a little. It’s something Evelyn Waugh would have done in a heartbeat. You’ve read *Bright Young Things*, haven’t you?”

Ravi blushed and took a moment to look deep into Mr. Darcy’s eyes. "It's actually called *Vile Bodies.* But, yes, the term *bright young things* does arise from the novel."

"And while you're at it, and when the time is right," he continued, ignoring Ravi, "you'll start writing some nice—how do you put it?—*items* about our young thing. You'll help to remake her image here, which will trickle down to the press in New York, which will drift to L.A. And all those blogs and glossy weeklies. But you'll make it happen. Do you see? How exciting will it be? It's a dream project."

"Does she need rehab? Does she have more issues than *Newsweek*?" Ravi asked. "As I said, I'm no Mary Poppins, and I'm no Promises rehab either."

"She doesn't have a drinking problem. She doesn't have a drug problem. And the only lines she's got these days are those she has to learn for an off-off-Broadway play she's doing in a few months, so she needs to be somewhere to concentrate. Somewhere fairly boring . . . like Toronto."

"Look," said Ravi, pausing for a second as rounds of bloody beef medallions were bequeathed to their table. "I know you've probably heard what Peter Ustinov said twenty years ago about this city—that Toronto is 'New York run by the Swiss'—but it's really not that dull anymore.

"It's changed," he defended with a certain asperity. "It's not just hockey. We have a world-class film festival, I'll have you know, where *tout* Hollywood comes. One year, both Bill Clinton and Brad Pitt came. And our big museum got a brow lift from world-class architect Daniel Libeskind. You do know, don't you, that Wolverine is Canadian?

"You do also know that *Chicago*, the Oscar-winning movie—Catherine Zeta-Jones! Renée Zellweger! Richard Gere!—was actually shot here," he clanged on, tossing around various other movies that featured American cities but were secretly Toronto. "*Cocktail* and *Mean Girls* and *Network* and *Hairspray* and . . ." He stopped for a minute, trying to think of another good example.

Ravi was mildly aware that he was beginning to sound like a mayoral candidate in the middle of a campaign, and Mr. Darcy, sitting back in his chair, feasted on him with a "whatever" look. Meanwhile, the repeated parroting of the term *world class* caused David Cronenberg, a few tables down, to crane his neck and magnify his ghoulish pout. Famous author and Gen-X messiah Douglas Coupland, who had just now entered the dining room—possibly to look for more demographic trends to make up clever buzzwords for—also took this moment to give a clarification-seeking look.

"Okay," Ravi finally gave up. "Just a few quick questions then."

Both men chewed for a bit, and the silence between them hung ominously.

"When will she—whoever she is—be here?"

"A week."

"And for how long?"

"A few months. Maybe more."

"How would this impact the rest of what I'm doing and my schedule?"

"It wouldn't. You take her along with you. Steer the girl, give her some class."

"In L.A., you told me you were a friend of Lady Ivory's. How?"

"Next question."

"Okay, how much are you paying me?"

"This much."

Mr. Darcy jotted down a number on a napkin—one that precisely jived with the ginormous figure that was Ravi's present debt load. Then, after giving Ravi a few more salient details, and filling him in on the identity of the little-known starlet, our self-described "operative" stood up, clicked his clogs, grabbed the one remaining bun for the road, and told Ravi that he'd be in touch.

The journalist didn't exactly say as much to Mr. Darcy then, but sitting in the creamy core of the Spoke Club, he'd pretty much made up his mind that he was going to take the job. He would call the man tomorrow. This, even though he had a hunch that he'd only been given half the story.

Why would he do it, when all was said and done? Well, the money didn't hurt. But it was money plus curiosity that was the most winning of combinations. And, really, had Ravi ever met a chandelier he didn't instinctively want to climb? He thought not. Moreover, as he would tell friends for years later, he did so because he had enough stars in his eyes and sufficient bile in his gut.

"Can I get you some coffee?" punctuated a waiter, interrupting his thoughts.

"No. Just some hot water will do."

6

Emergency Bon Mots

"You have to be really careful when you're cleaning art. My ex-husband has a Rothko—he got the Rothko and I got the kids, you see—and there was a slight tear, and they had to call in a conservator from London to tie each individual fibre back into its place. It's a process called *rissverklebung*. I know, I know, leave it to the Germans! Ha! I mean, can you imagine? *Every* single fibre? Goodness, I get impatient just having my highlights put in!"

A mealy-mouthed society hausfrau, adrift in the hurly-burly of her oratory, had in her snare a pastels-preferring octogenarian. This, at an art dinner that sought Ravi's command performance the very eve before the Plan, hatched at the Spoke with Mr. Darcy, was designed to wind. Phone calls had come and gone; the ins and outs of the mission looped.

The woman was still talking: "It's like when Steve Wynn, the casino mogul—my current husband and I always stay at the Wynn when we're in Vegas—he ripped a hole through his $140 million

Picasso painting. You heard about that, didn't you? I read an article that said it happened while Wynn was gesticulating at a cocktail party, showing off the painting. Can you imagine? *Gesticulating,* they said! Clearly, he's not German. Apparently, the hole was the size of a toonie. Can you imagine? And he was in the middle of selling the Picasso, and then—can you imagine?—the deal was off. Just like that."

"I guess that it was time then for Steve Wynn's own Blue Period, no?" interrupted Ravi.

Having noticed that the man on the receiving end of this stirring monologue was starting, very visibly, to doze off, he had taken it upon himself to swoop in with an Emergency Bon Mot. (When used both effectively and swiftly, the Emergency Bon Mot, not unlike an emergency airlift of food, can buy time, offer a way out, aid the suffering. It is commonly used not in Burma or Cambodia, but at art dinners or book launches or store openings, where some people are known to ransack a party with their prose, their anecdotes, their ever-so-scintillating opinions.)

With the garrulous woman stopped in her tracks, and the conversation given a chance to breathe—just like a good wine—the drowsy darling was allowed to adjust his body and begin a conversation anew with the hobbity gentleman on his other side. Ravi, who was across from both these people, let out a humanitarian sigh and felt, for but a moment, like Queen Rania or Angelina Jolie or Bono. At which point, he sprinkled some celebratory Emergen-C into his Fiji Water.

The dinner that night was one of the regular art gatherings that Judy Firkin liked to throw in her barn-sized gallery in a cobblestoned area in the east end of the city for fifty, give or take, of her closest friends/potential collectors. The scene, falling down in strokes as if by a Jackson Pollock flip, was offset by giant candles ("chamomile-scented," a fellow diner had told Ravi, because apparently this induces certain pheromones that cause spontaneous art buying) but *not* offset by flowers because, as Judy, who looked like a grown-up version of Lisa Simpson, had put it to him earlier, all and any buds were banned. ("With all the art here," she had plainly pointed out, "we don't need them.") The lighting, he had to say, truly was spot-on, reminding him of one of the maxims of that oldest of old-school society hostesses Elsa Maxwell. The keys to throwing a good dinner party, she'd said, were to provide good lighting and to baby the guests, treating them as if they were children all over again.

Looking down on his truffle-oil oxtail ravioli accompanied by saffron-and-mint-speckled stuffed New Zealand quail and a goblet-busters Merlot from Dan Aykroyd's winery, Ravi wondered exactly how many of these dinners he had been to in his life as an official swan-abouter and why he was not as bothered as he should be about being at yet another. Either he had a special gift for self-torture or he really was enamoured of the fabulousness (even when it was Japanese-paper-thin), by the tap-tap of social ambition (even when it led to bathos), and by the idea of figuring out all those people who, on any given night, at any given party were trying to reconcile their real selves with their purported halves.

"What do you think of the work?"

A man with windburnt cheeks—one of those guys whose actual source of income remained a matter that would have stumped both Agatha Christie and Jessica Fletcher, and who seemed to go out every night like his life depended on it—was the one who wanted to know. Rumour had it that this gold-medal brown-noser kept quite detailed dossiers on the "important people" around town. Some people, quite a lot actually, said he was charming. Ravi felt that these people weren't very good judges of charm. At the moment, the brown-noser was asking the requisite art question while a sundry of after-dinner digestifs went around.

"I find it . . . derivative," Ravi answered, pausing in such a way that his words came out with an elaborate insouciance.

"Yes. Michael Snow did it all in the 1960s, didn't he?" answered back Mr. Windburnt Cheeks, promptly excusing himself to go talk to one of the guys who'd created the board game Trivial Pursuit, who, in turn, was talking to one of the Barenaked Ladies, who, in turn, was talking to a woman who looked like local neo-hippie songbird Feist but was actually a woman with bangs who only looked like Feist.

Derivative seemed to always do the trick at these events, Ravi smiled to himself, lingering on the word. He had first heard Diane Keaton churn out the term in the movie *Manhattan.* It was a scene where she and Woody Allen—so young and so fantastically black and white—were walking on the street, having just come from a show in the gallery. It was the kind of word that was vague enough to be always useful and tidy enough to be often instructive. Perfect for a party!

When it came around to after-dinner drinks, the action shifted to the upper floor, where around the artist, one Mr. Ji-Min Na—born Jason Nixon in Prince Edward Island, until an inspiring trip to Jakarta turned him into the man he was—stood an admiring armada of art buffs. In that circle, Ravi gladly noted, was expert equestrian and incorrigible globetrotter Bruce Bailey, standing next to one of those Lululemon socialites who, rumour had it, had a severely overweight Jack Russell terrier at home and, rumour further had it, had managed to get so incredibly skunked one night at And/Or that she'd come into the men's room and upchucked some nori sushi into a urinal.

Beside Ms. Nobu and the equestrian/globetrotter was celebrity academic Harvey Delaware. One of the most hyped-up eggheads of his generation, with the Johnny Depp dimples to match, he was an authority on fonts and their "interplay with civilization." He and his model-perfect wife, Gita, had earned the love and love-hate of the city since their triumphant arrival two years ago, and at this particular moment he was expounding generously on Arial Narrow Bold.

Tugging at this circle now were three power couples, and each component of every power couple seemed to be doing its job. It went something like this: someone (in this case, the artist) would ask one of the strangers in the crowd what they did, at which point the person being asked would say, "Oh, not much" or something else proto-bashful, after which point the spouse (or such) of the stranger would begin a monologue like this: "Oh, *Michael* (or fill in the blank) just sold his company for $126 million and was just interviewed about it on *Report on Business TV*, and he loves Château Margaux—he has more than one in his collection, I'll just say—and did you know that Wayne Gretzky inaugurated the skating rink we just put in our backyard?"

Not long ago, Ravi had read somewhere that being in a relationship was like having a full-time publicist, and these days, frankly, he saw it everywhere. In order to be suitably demure about one's accomplishments and maintain a who-me? sense of decorum, one's wife or husband or girlfriend or boyfriend did all the listing and all the bragging on one's behalf. Having someone who loved you, or loved you enough to go to parties with you, was, in other words, like an actor who had a "personal," as was the casually used term for those handholding Hollywood PR types.

Having a plus-one? Just another word for having PR.

He also couldn't help but notice that when one component of a couple here asked another component of a second couple how they were, the second person responded, quick as a pistol, "Busy." This, too, was not very surprising. Ravi wasn't exactly sure when it became customary to give the answer "busy" when people asked, "How are you?" but he guessed it must have been back around the time that Kathleen Turner was getting lead roles in movies. More and more he saw it: people who, when met with acquaintances and friends alike, instead of knocking off a perfunctory "Fine, thank you" or a faux-chummy "I'm hanging in there" or even the old "Not bad" to the question coughed up a pat and beige "Busy," usually aiding the one-word answer with a nice microwaveable smile.

It was not a response. It was a post-modern boast. Saying you're busy these days was a bit like saying in a job interview that the worst thing about you is that you're a perfectionist. The boast was sly, but it was still a boast. *Busy,* really, had climbed up there with *smart* and *funny* on the list of adjectives you would like others to pick when describing yourself. You could, it seems, never be too rich or too thin or too busy.

If you're not busy, there might be something wrong with you, so you never forgot to tell people that you were busy. You're drowning in work. Your hands are full. You're swamped. And lunch? Who has time to have lunch anymore?

It had been Ravi's experience, though, that the people who crocodile-teared about being busy were so not. Unless you were Rupert Murdoch or Richard Branson or Jay-Z or, well, an assorted handful of others, you weren't really busy. You were stretched by your own doing, perhaps, or just plain neglectful, or lying to yourself, or just using the "busy pretence" to get out of doing certain things, but you weren't really time-totalled. Let's face it: even presumably very busy people such as Bill Clinton could figure out ways to, um, fit in certain things if they really wanted to. Busyness, in this respect, wasn't really about all the stuff you have to do. It was a sign of success; the snap of social hierarchy. It was the noise that hotshots make.

Just as he was considering this particular thesis on the Art of Busy, a vibration tingled up from his well-lined, gift-lounge-provided J. Lindeberg blazer. It was a text on his phone from dear, dear Rory, and it went pretty much like this: Where are U? Call Me! I'M YOUR WIFE, DAMIT!!!

Ravi, who hated texting and often wished he had a texting sherpa, fingered back this pithy reply: Shall call U soon. I'm having a heart to art. Terribly fondly, Ravi.

At this point, after he'd exchanged social softballs with a

gourmand power widow whose daughter had recently noun-ed her way into a dude, courtesy of surgery, the woman who was throwing the party zeroed in on the journalist putting away his mobile and stalked right over to ask whether he had met everyone he needed to—which was just another way of asking if he was going to mention her lots and lots when he wrote up his column. He lied to Judy Firkin and said he had talked to just about everyone, knowing full well that at this particular arc in his career, he could go to one of these parties both blindfolded and with earplugs in and later still write it up in such a decorous way that few out there would be able to tell the difference.

"We have another dinner next month. I'll send you the deets," she said to him, practically following him out the door as he tried to flee. Her cheeks were betraying a certain pink. "Feel free to bring your, um, partner. If you have a partner, that is, or"—chuckling fast now—"well, one, in particular, I should say. Even if you don't, that also works! A guy like you probably has a few dance partners! *Que sera, sera,* like I always say. Thank you so much for coming! It was really so kind of you. Say, can I get you a cab?"

Once he had successfully left the party, Ravi walked quietly along King Street toward the part of town where the towers loomed longingly, squatted selfishly, and, in a way, filled out the crevices of his and others' lives.

Looking at the gizmo-seeming skyscrapers—in particular, the Mies van der Rohe–designed TD Tower that he counted as his favourite—Ravi thought of the place that was his oyster. A city of four-odd million people that was, by most measures, the nation's commercial-cultural capital, Toronto wasn't the Swiss-influenced place of its early reputation but more likely, and temperamentally, like some ying-and-yang yoke of New York and, say, Stockholm.

He had, like most people, come to this continent as an immigrant. But rather than hurt his head by thinking too much about that, or get too Toni Morrison or Rohinton Mistry on the subject, he began to demark the place in celebrity terms. It was a common game of his. Somewhere out there in this very city, Ravi began to muse, there was Kiefer Sutherland's hell-raising mother, Shirley Douglas, putting on her night eye-cream and getting ready for bed, as were perhaps the parents of David Furnish, a chap who had lucked out and hit the absolute gay jackpot by marrying one Elton John. As was Nelly Furtado, who did her man-eating in the city.

Somewhere out there, he thought, there were streets—maybe even this one—that Joni Mitchell had once tread, somewhere around the time that she started singing about paved paradises, and that prophetic guru Marshall McLuhan, who came up with all that stuff about mediums and messages and global villages, and, also, of course, Frank Gehry, who put the star in starchitect, and Nia Vardalos, who put the big, fat, and Greek in wedding. Jim Carrey and Eugene Levy. Mike Myers and Martin Short. Will from *Will & Grace* and that bald guy from *Deal or No Deal.* Oh, and that interestingly haired brainiac from *The New Yorker* who came up with the tipping point. Not to mention Darth Vader, a.k.a. Hayden Christensen, and Neo from *The Matrix,* a.k.a. Keanu Reeves. And even, yes, culture-catching editors like Tyler Brûlé, that self-invented fancy-pants known best for whipping up *Wallpaper**, and Bonnie Fuller, that particularly talented tabloidist who, like the others, had once both plotted and plodded here.

His thoughts turned to this funny, neurotic sprawl of a country. The one that had managed to produce both suavest of suaves, like the late anchorman Peter Jennings, but also the stoniest of stoners, like the au courant Seth Rogen. The country that, as ironies would have it, was responsible for both American Apparel and America's Sweetheart: the first being a hipster-outfitting, deep-V-neck-propagating chain (founded, naturally, by a Canadian) and the latter being the very first movie star—a.k.a. the silent era's Mary Pickford. Not so widely known was the fact that old Mary hailed from these northern environs.

And somewhere out there, getting ready to descend on him and the whole funny, glittering, consuming place, was She. The special project, c/o Mr. Darcy. She. Leeza Pellegrino. That was her name.

Tomorrow, Ravi thought. Tomorrow.

7

The Only Bad Publicity Is Your Obituary?

"Is there a Balenciaga?"

Those were the four words that first came out of Leeza Pellegrino, beautiful brunette, would-be starlet, age twenty-two. The sliding door into the Hazelton Hotel, where the meeting had been arranged, had barely open-sesame-ed all the way before she'd gone and spooled her first question mark.

"I'm assuming that's not a rhetorical question," Ravi responded. He rose from the Karim Rashid Oh Chair on which he had been idling with his laptop and, smiling passive-aggressively, he offered his hand.

Ms. Pellegrino, who obviously had an actress's innate sense of how to make an entrance, had lips so red they looked like a British postbox, and her hair was nothing if not sarcastic. Like that of someone who had just arisen from a hammock—but a hammock located on Turtle Island or in St. Barts. That is to say, in the fuller analysis, she made messy work for her. Her stockings had more holes than James Frey's life story, her big, bad shoes were evidently stolen from Minnie's boudoir, and her babydoll frock seemed to be partly inspired by Jean Seberg and partly by Stevie Nicks but had come out in the wash as Wilma Flintstone. In sum, her look drew far too heavily on Mary-Kate and Ashley's famous "Dumpster Chic," as labelled by a famous *New York Times* article from a few years ago. So much so that Ravi was almost tempted to abduct this child right away and deposit her at the nearest meeting of Fashion Victims Anonymous.

"There is no standalone Balenciaga store here," he told her, making sure to use the tone a gentle doc might use when informing his patient that he may just have discovered a tumour.

The young thing, with an apparent knack for switching the subject, answered, "My name is Leeza Pellegrino. Pellegrino like the water; Leeza with a zee. Or since we're in Canada now and you have those weird spellings, Leeza with a zed."

At this point, Ravi felt his stomach rumble. Either that or it was the triumphant thump of his IQ dropping.

Or was it?

As the day went on it, it began to dawn on him that his new charge, Leeza, might just have a zigzag circuitry up there in that gorgeous head of hers. And that's *zigzag* with two zeds. If Jackie Collins was describing this, Ravi thought, she might put it like this: There's more to this girl than meets the Ray-Bans!

After both of them had checked into their respective rooms (Mr. Darcy had suggested he stay at the hotel during the span of their operation, a proposition that was not met with resistance by Ravi) and after they'd made off for a quick bite at Café Doria on Yonge Street, she outright stunned him by making a nimble reference to Indo-Pakistani politics. It came in between bites of a panini, which she chewed extra, extra slowly, as was the metabolistic inclination among many a Hollywooder (including Angelina Jolie, whom Ravi had once spent a whole lunchtime watching in a restaurant. She chewed and she chewed. It went on for hours).

I was dating this guy, blah, blah, blah, Leeza had started to say, and we were so in love, blah, blah, blah, but his parents didn't like me, blah, blah, blah, and my parents didn't like him, "and then it was like Partition . . . 1947 all over again, y'know?"

Yes, Ravi did know. His posture stiffened, though he managed to nod. He knew that not *every* gift-bag-collecting, red-carpet-strolling, Nobu-stopping-in would-be-starlet went around dropping casual mentions to the decades-old, geopolitical mark in the road between India and Pakistan. It just didn't happen. Not even in the case of Ms. Pellegrino, who, to the extent of his casual reading of the tabs over the years, and his more targeted research of late, had served time on a critically unacclaimed sitcom for half a season, was not famous enough to get a spot on *Dancing with the Stars*, not famous enough to get even fifteen minutes on *Larry King*, and, more poignantly, was now one of the hundreds, if not thousands, of wannabes toiling in bit-part movieland.

As a tiny drop of pesto trickled its way down the side of Leeza's mouth, and that mouth then worked its way into a classic get-out-of-jail-free-card smile, Ravi, for the first time, got a sense of what he was up against. Ravi, whose job it was to read people, saw the prepossessing lip curl that comes naturally to those who feel that the only bad publicity to be had is one's obituary. It is a beam that belongs to those who do know they can get away with anything. Could it be that sitting beside him was a panini-eating princess with the metabolism of Suzanne Somers, the theatrics of Susan Lucci, and, oh, the plotting prowess of Sue Grafton?

The 1947 Partition comment told him a couple things, for starters. One, she was obviously trying to speak to his ethnicity without deliberately bringing it up, i.e., telegraph the message that she was "down with it." (Just like the time, come to think of it, when he was in the home of an Important Socialite and, out of nowhere, mid-conversation, she had begun to rave to him about the "wonders" of yoga and the "colours" of Rajasthan). Two, the mere fact that Leeza was canny enough to try this trick—obvious as it was—suggested she was no conveyor-belt bimbo. That she was canny enough to try this trick confirmed that she was at least willing to do her research.

And, well, did it not take one to know one? It did. Was it not just like the time Ravi met Morgan Freeman during the Toronto Film Festival and just *happened* to mention to him that his contemporary—one Samuel Jackson—was encroaching on his turf with a new audio version of the Bible in which he played the voice of God (as Freeman had first done in the movie *Bruce Almighty*)? Which just *happened* to give Ravi enough reaction to spoon out an entire column.

"I'm glad it's him!" Morgan had joked back when informed about the Lordly-come-lately.

"Yes," Ravi replied, continuing with the ha-ha. "You wouldn't want to get typecast as God." He then swiftly followed up by telling him, "Jackson is here, actually."

"At this party?" Morgan made the inquiry in his familiar baritone.

No, no, Ravi came back. In Toronto for the festival. "He's been at every party," he exaggerated.

"He wouldn't dare come here," Freeman countered.

At which point, Morgan and Ravi had looked at each other pensively and decided that this conversation was getting just a little too weird. Both sighing sighs of resignation, they backed away mutually, like extras in a musical.

The *point* being, the God-talk hadn't been spur of the moment at all but concocted and pointed and calculated, based on research that Ravi had done before going to that particular party. (Because, after all, the art of being a gossip columnist was to make it look like there was no art and to be as natural as possible, but, meanwhile, behind in the shadows, it took scads of research and all manner of non-stop "keeping up" with the news, the trends, the passing seasons of pop culture.)

The *point* being there was nothing idle here about Leeza throwing out some ancient subcontinental history. And then, a little later, nothing altogether off the cuff about her quoting David Sedaris. Yes, she was parroting. But at least she knew whom to parrot. It was the thing W. Somerset Maugham once attributed to one of his characters: “She had a pretty gift for quotation, which is a serviceable substitute for wit.” Ravi, for one, always gave full points to people who parroted well. If stealing opinions were so easy, wouldn’t more people have more opinions?

Not to say there weren’t overt signs of flightiness in this rogue woman-child. There was, for instance, her very palpable problem with air quotes. In the span of an hour, he saw the young thing use air quotes at least three times, putting up fingers behind her head in inverted-commas mode to communicate the irony, or thereabouts, of what she was saying. Once when she said something about being an “actress” (a fact, thus far, Ravi really couldn’t dispute) and another time when she used the word *I*.

Again, perhaps most disturbingly, when she asked the waiter for a “latte.”

“A latte?” asked the poor guy, not twice-twitching his fore and second fingers to go along with the word.

“Yes,” she sniffed, giving Ravi an is-he-deaf-or-what? look.

“Did you know that you air-quoted when you asked for your latte?” Ravi thought it was best to bring up the subject right away, using the same reasoning he would apply if he saw a friend park in a no-park zone. The air-quote bonanza had begun, he recalled, with Generation X but had become an unstoppable and increasingly misused habit with the kids that followed. Britney Spears, for one, was one of the worst transgressors, having once infamously air-quoted her way through a TV chat with Matt Lauer.

“What do you mean?”

“You so air-quoted!”

"Did not!"

"Did so."

"Did I?" she then asked, gasping.

"Unless you were asking for some of British Columbia's finest hippie lettuce instead of a regular old latte, I don't think air quotes are really necessary."

This got the requisite laugh out of Leeza, and with it, both of them decided that they had bonded.

"Confession," she retorted after a few beats. "I air-quote a lot, but I really air-quote a lot when I'm nervous. I guess I'm a little nervous."

"And I'm guessing we have our guesswork cut out for us," he said, not knowing exactly what that meant but thinking it sounded pretty pithy. Next: "What are you nervous about?"

"Just this whole thing," she said. "I know I'm supposed to hang with you a bit, and you're supposed to help me get my act together. It just feels kind of like we're in a reality show, but we're not, you know what I mean?"

Ravi nodded thoughtfully.

After the journalist and the actress had epilogued their lunch with a round of coffees, and after they'd gotten to know each other a little better, and after they'd successfully circled the subject of what her visit to town was all about, they left Café Doria and walked out onto a bright, sunny Yonge Street. Across the street, there was a Starbucks, and an accompanying outside patio, where sat a man who looked to be . . .

"Hey, isn't that, like, David Cronenberg?" Leeza exclaimed, her hair falling freely about her shoulders.

It was the white-and-green-cup-accessorized auteur, indeed. Appearing before Ravi for the second time in just a few days. As they slowly and deliberately promenaded by him, he thought, What a small town this sometimes is, ain't it just? A thought that was then shadowed by this additional lingering thought: So, this airhead knows her auteurs, does she?

8

Voulez-vous du champagne?

Was Leeza Pellegrino a handful?

Put it this way:

Did Whitney Houston ever happen to employ the words *love, will, always,* and *you* on *The Bodyguard* soundtrack?

Did Evita ever do Dior?

Did Damien Hirst dig formaldehyde?

Does double-sided tape sell well in Hollywood? (Or, for that matter, do Spanx?)

Does Missoni do stripes?

Is Capri pretty?

Did the War of 1812 take place in 1812?

Yes, Leeza Pellegrino was a handful. And incorrigible. And, at times, being with her was like climbing Machu Picchu with Rosie O'Donnell hoisted on your back. But in the week that followed—which followed yet another week—Ravi grew both exasperated and enchanted with this creature who'd been parachuted into his life.

He was, after all, a lifelong admirer and student of Difficult Women.

She made a wonderful date, he found out soon enough. Except when she didn't. At one of those uptown galas that often found *him*—the kind where the men arrive in 007 suits and the women have bloodsucker mouths and there's always a hell of a lot of endangered sea bass to go around—Leeza charmed the gala chair to tickles when she got behind one of the surging bars and swiftly (and without any prodding) began playing very efficient backup to an overextended bartender.

"Wherever did you ever find her?" an appreciative Wanda Tapperdash exclaimed to Ravi later, as one of Wanda's many minions—a woman known around town as the Shiksa Non Grata—backed her up.

"A friend of a fiend," Ravi replied, which got the intended oh-you cackle out of Ms. Tapperdash and an echo-cackle out of the Shiksa Non Grata. Later that same night, he watched Leeza make the time to have meaningful small talk with an earth-tones-wearing nonagenarian sitting all by his lonesome.

It was a different scene, however, when Ravi trotted her out for a dinner held at Nota Bene in honour of Mary Jo Eustace, who was what they called a "personality" these days. Famously, she'd hosted a number of TV shows in this country. Infamously, she had had her name intertwined forever with Tori Spelling when the Flaxen Hollywood Princess stole her husband—whose name escapes us. Tonight, Mary Jo was launching a new line of organic grapes. "Not Sour" was her slogan. "Thanks for coming, Ravi," she said to her old pal, smiling her cubist smile. At which point, Ravi introduced dear Leeza. At which point, dear Leeza took Mary Jo's hand and asked, "So, like, do you know Jason Priestly?" That didn't go over particularly well.

Certainly, it wasn't that much prettier when he took her to the launch of something or another held at Lee, on King Street. She wore a purple-grape itty-bitty number that trod the line between merely inappropriate and almost sluttish, to match a voice that seemed to vary always between almost kittenish and merely SoCal. After the first course was presented—Susur Lee's celebrated slaw made of nineteen different kinds of cabbage—she proceeded to give her review to the superstar cook. She told him that she loved the dish, except that she found it too "cabbage-y." Then, admiring the chef's signature ponytail, she asked if she could pull it.

"Well, since you asked—" he began to say. And so, pull she did.

Basically, Leeza was like the Canadian weather. You just never knew what you were going to get. Some days: cloudy with a ninety percent chance of crazy. On others: morning fog patches, with a high near lovely.

But into Ravi's world she went, and by all accounts, she seemed to be enjoying all the kiss-and-tell, the skullduggery and the scene-chewing, the vain and vacuous splendour. "But how do you remember all the names?" she exclaimed one day after a sporty few hours of browsing at Holt Renfrew.

"Alliteration," he told her, stopping her in the aisles of the fancy vortex. "And if you really want to play in the big leagues, Leeza, you have to get this down too. If you meet a Louisa, think

Lardy Louisa. If you're introduced to a Sebastian, say to yourself, Saucy Sebastian."

"How do I get people to take me more seriously?" she asked on another occasion, as they sat watching a molten sun from the venerable rooftop bar at the Park Hyatt. In the corner, he caught the auspiciously jawlined J.D. Roberts, who for many years during his American interlude at CBS and CNN was known as John Roberts but was rumoured to be returning triumphantly to Canada to anchor the country's biggest newscast and reverting, on cue, to his original homespun initials.

"Well, that, my darling, is simple," no-frilled Ravi, whipping out a simple black notebook with a simple elastic closure. "Just make sure you carry around one of these Moleskines along with your PDA. This is the legendary notebook that was carried by everyone from Matisse to van Gogh to Ernest Hemingway. A few years ago, it was rebooted as a brand, and since then it's become a kind of secret handshake among deep-thinking people.

"Really?" she said, caressing the notebook.

"You're either a Moleskiner or you're not, Leeza," he went on. "You are. As of now. Just be sure to be seen making coy little notes whenever you're in public. People will think you're deeply mysterious."

Waiting for further instructions or, at the very least, a smoke signal from Mr. Darcy, or Mr. Anybody, he kept the young missus occupied by doing a lot more of what seemed to come most naturally to her: shopping. When he wasn't helping *her* help the local economy, he left her to work on the play she was supposed to be appearing in a few months later. During this time, they continued to avoid (and circle) any in-depth conversations about the whole purpose of their bunk-up together (as advised by Mr. Darcy), and instead he entertained her with a home-school program made up of classic old movies.

"It's good for you," he'd tell Leeza, as he made a point of showing her, say, *The Apartment,* with the madcap Shirley MacLaine, or, on yet another day, *Now, Voyager,* starring the ferocious Bette Davis.

Ah, yes. Speaking of Difficult Women. . .

The good news too? Her air-quote recovery seemed to be proceeding well. It had taken a while, but she was now down to only several finger-flings a day. And where this precise flinging was concerned, even that had improved. But Leeza, he'd noticed, tended to use a variety of fingers and was inconsistent about the height of her air quotes.

"If you're going to air-quote, you're going to at least air-quote well," he told her. "Look at this," he said, showing her something he'd tracked down on the Internet about how to do so properly. "You use this form of communication," he read out loud, "when stating something that is from a source other than yourself or to artificially distance yourself from your own stupid opinions."

Keeping at her one day as they took a walk down St. Clair Avenue, past the apartment where the great, long-gone pianist Glenn Gould once played his scales and housed his neuroses, Ravi recited air-quote instructions from his BlackBerry: "Hold up both hands, palms facing away from you and slightly forward of vertical, with the pinky and ring fingers curled into the palms, leaving the middle and index fingers relatively straight and pointing up and away from you." He paused for effect, then said, "The thumbs should remain relaxed."

"Like this?" she asked, poising her hands in the air as urged.

"Better," confirmed Ravi.

"Now," he continued. "The final part of the gesture is to simultaneously curl the middle and index fingers of both hands about halfway to the closed position. Normally twice."

Since, though, he did have a life—and it was a life that consisted mainly of reporting on other people's lives—the show needed to go on. One that involved more than Turner Classic Movies and air-quote amelioration.

"Guess what? We're going to a comedy festival! In Montreal!" This is what he announced out of the blue as the young Pellegrino sat at a vanity table, robotically straightening her hair.

She didn't speak for a bit, apparently not wanting to lose focus on her task at hand. Having watched the young thing do this a few times, and having had it explained to him in intricate terms, he knew she was somewhere in the middle of a process that began with working a balm through the hair from roots to ends (combing through thoroughly to ensure even distribution); then smoothing it all out using a "paddle brush"; following that, flat-ironing it "section by section"; and, last but not least, smoothing it all over with a drop of silicone-based shine-enhancing serum to give one's locks an extra *je ne sais quoi.*

"It's important to start ironing as close as possible to the roots for the sleekest finish," Leeza had explained to him one day in beauty-mag speak.

Now she simply said, "Okay." And then, "What I really need right now, though, is a manicure. If I don't, the cuticle police are going to come get us."

Knowing that cuticles always come before comedy, Ravi acceded to the demand but told her she should be ready to leave for Montreal—a short flight—in three hours to catch the evening's festivities at Just for Laughs, that city's annual festival. Or, as those laugh-out-loud French called it, Juste Pour Rire. In both of Canada's official languages, it translated into the world's most important cackle convention, to which comics came, from far and from wide, to deliver their lines, pull their punches, and dream big, blazing dreams of a sitcom deal.

Leaving her to her devices, Ravi retired to his room and, ripping off his clothes, rushed to make that day's column deadline. (Naked being his preferred state when it came to writing.) On tap for that day, among other things, he had:

Peter Gatien, the one-eyed former New York club lord. Having been exiled to Canada, he had been making noises of late about opening another club here called Definitive. Somewhere during the country transfer, he'd abandoned his signature eyepatch, though, and had now reverted simply to wearing blue-tinted sunglasses.

Mummy boy Brendan Fraser. Having long harboured a non-Napoleonic complex as the rare tall man in Hollywood, the Canadian now suffered from "bad posture," as he had recently revealed in an interview. "It's my natural inclination to be diminutive and stoop, so as to not feel I'm dominating. I've always had a complex about being six-two."

Lord Ivory, the troubled titan. Having landed squarely in court, courtesy of his financial pickle, his woes had now caused him to have to sell off the Catherine the Great serving spoons he had in his collection, as well as the auction-worthy vintage London cab he kept in the garage for occasional runs to the 7-Eleven.

Okay, what else? Ravi racked his brain. Exactly what was that tip that had come through from a publicist at the Food Network, the one tacitly encouraging him to mention Nigella Lawson's latest show? The well-enunciating Domestic Goddess had passed through town, and the flack in question knew that Ravi would gladly do a plug for the show if she gave Ravi something to hang his story on. This was, of course, how it worked. So, after jogging his memory just so, he, like Stravinsky, approached his keyboard and began banging out the words:

"I see, I hear that buxom braiser Nigella Lawson, in town recently promoting her greatest and latest new Food Network show, *Nigella Bares All*, was spotted at Joso's on Davenport the other night. Out with her that night? The not-so-known but oh-so-powerful Hettie Potter!"

"Hettie," he went on, "is Nigella's right-hand woman, my sources tell me. Quite literally, in that, in many instances, her hands actually sub in for the British cook's in photo shoots. In addition to doing hand stunts, Hettie's duties include recipe tasting! Nice work if you can you-know-what!"

While he was writing, a man from room service appeared at his door, bearing something that looked too good. Before he'd had a chance to tell him, no, he actually hadn't ordered anything, he noticed the note—complete with out-of-central-casting flower—that lay lovingly on the tray.

"In case you forget to stop for lunch while you're working. Love, Leeza," it read. Just the kind of touch that, in one fabulous full swoop, attested again to the notion that there was more to our Leeza than sleek finishes and nail preservation.

"P.S.," went the note, "Remember: Comedy is tragedy plus time." Boy, did this girl do her research! Sometimes!

"Knock, knock."

Ravi did not need to turn around to find out that the voice in the bar behind him belonged to his one-and-only Rory. But he did.

"Who's there?" she went on, playing both parts in this familiar exchange. "It's your friggin' wife!"

"How nice to meet you," he quipped in return.

Here in this city bursting with fits of braying laughter, and much more brazen street eye contact, the not-so-old ball and chain had managed to track him down. Typical.

"I had to come all the way to Montreal to find you."

"Well, bienvenue."

"Ravi, we really need to talk about where this is going."

"Careful, Rory, you're beginning to sound bourgeois."

"Careful, Ravi, you're about to have your crown jewels cut off."

"Oh, my sweetie-pie darling-doll, can't you just chillax a little?"

"No, my macaroon, I will not chillax! And don't you dare tell me to be more Zenful either!"

"Who are you, George Foreman? What's with the grillin', baby? I know, why don't we go to a nice café somewhere—perhaps L'Express—where we can eat good croque monsieurs and watch some separatists and, well, talk about all of this?"

"Ravi, I don't want a croque monsieur, and I don't wear berets, and I don't want to talk . . ."

"You just said you wanted to talk."

"When I said we needed to talk, I meant I was going to deliver a monologue and you were going to obey! Don't you know anything about gender relations?"

Her voice must have echoed a little too loud because here in this St. Laurent bar that was basically comic ground zero there was, all of a sudden, much turning of heads. Various deadpan funnymen, drenched in Drakkar Noir, looked up. So, too, it might as well be mentioned, did a few terribly funny ladies who, clearly, very clearly, had not been Sephora-housebroken yet.

Ravi flashed all of them a smile, as if to say, Carry on. She's just kidding, of course. This is a comedy festival, after all! His wife—who was never sexier than when she was mad, he had to admit—reciprocated by sidling right up to his face and saying, "We need to get to a point where you're not phoning in your spousal performance."

Then who should appear . . . but young Leeza.

"Ravi, I totally think I saw Lorne Michaels coming out of the washroom," she gurgled, looking slightly coquettish in jeans, cropped blazer, and a Scope-coloured tee that read, Save Darfur. The last he'd seen her, she'd been in another part of the bar having her flesh eye-devoured by several horny cut-ups.

"I highly doubt Mr. Michaels, the father of *Saturday Night Live* and Canadian comic genius, does either one or two in a public washroom," Rory informed the innocent. "And who are you?"

"Leeza, meet Rory," Ravi rushed in. He added, by way of playful interjection, "She's my insignificant other."

"Rory," he then said, turning to the new bride in his life, "this is Leeza. Leeza, with a zed. She's sort of my Eliza Doolittle these days. Eliza with a zed."

Because Ravi was known for speaking in a particular manner, and sometimes in a code that many people only pretended to understand, neither woman could be bothered to react to the description of the other. It was one of the benefits of being a boy who so often cried coy.

And, today, as he was clearly on thin Canadian ice, our man skated like Kurt Browning around the twin identities of both women meeting for the first time, all the while trying to keep track of the little white lies falling on that ice and slowly but assuredly leading the talk to the small and innocuous variety.

Minutes into it, however, just about the time that Leeza had begun to ask Rory, "So, how do you know Ravi?" our skillful small-talker clapped his hands, stood up, and announced that the three of them needed to split this joint.

"Mon Dieu, I totally forgot! There's a chic comedy soiree I need to get to! Vite, vite! Taxi, s'il vous plait!"

Thus, it wasn't all that much later when Ravi, secret wife and confidential starlet in tow, found himself in a penthouse just a little less hot than Naomi Campbell's head and one with a pretty sizeable largesse of hot chicks. *'Ot,* as some of the more charming, *h*-challenged natives would put it.

There they were with their Louvre-worthy painted toes and their Brazilian-waxed surfaces, their bodies as slick and supple as Philippe Starck juicers. Some of them looked like the kind of gals who had experience with men who gave gift cards for Christmas. A comic he recognized—one who appeared to be into his second trimester but had the confidence of a matador—was surrounded by at least four of them. Daniel Lanois, the famous music producer, was in on it too.

And on the outskirts of those outskirts? A no-stranger-to-Montreal Rufus Wainwright, whose partiality lay with songs made for drowning oneself in the bathtub. (Was his presence here in these comic parts a sign that he was trying to broaden his fan base? Perhaps, perhaps.)

"What kind of comedy show is this anyways?" asked Rory, as the unlikely trio made their entrance. "Is David Beckham doing stand-up now?"

"I smell frenemies," whispered Leeza, taking a quick peek around the room.

"It's not a comedy show," muttered Ravi. "At least not that kind." Then, because he always had a sixth sense for the party behind the party, he shepherded his troupe to the massive balcony, which offered a vantage point for Montreal's polite neon and, if one peered farther, a view of the massively illuminated cross on top of Mont Royal. As usual, it was playing its role as omnipresent landmark, beaming whiter than Meryl Streep's hair in *The Devil Wears Prada.*

"Champagne?" announced three different waiters at once, pouring and shoving one, two, three glasses into their reach.

"Ravi, really," tried Rory again. "What is this?"

He was just about to explain when a woman (one with a man-did-I-tie-one-on-last-night face) manifested and began speaking into a microphone. "Mesdames et messieurs," she said in her implacable, official-language French before switching to a more-than-passable English. "My name is Yvette. I'm so happy you could be here. As you know, it's the first time we've had a presence at Just for Laughs, but we thought it was important for us to reach out to the comedic community."

Rory stared at Ravi, who shrugged to Leeza.

"The comedic community," the Yvette lady repeated, pausing, "is very important to us and, historically, to civilization's funny-bone." She got the *h* in *historically*, Ravi noticed. "And, in many ways our raison d'être, shall we say, is similar to yours. We are, after all, both in the business of bubbles. And we both make people tickle. It is with my great pleasure then that we are here to inaugurate this new special champagne—Rire—which will help to mark a new chapter in the co-operation between champagne and comedy." She raised her glass, gave a wily glance, and, before clinking into the air, announced pseudo-gravely, "Vive le champagne!"

"Vive le champagne," roared about half the crowd. The other part, Ravi noticed, was still deep in the burrows of chit-chat.

"So, comedians are the new hip-hoppers?" Rory summed up. "Champagne's latest target group."

"That Judd Apatow has a lot to answer for," answered Ravi. "He's evidently created a new market outreach opportunity."

Leeza, up for a laugh, was by now off and talking to a hot comedian from Korea, "the Jim Carrey of Seoul," as he was called. Rory, on the other hand, had just begun to try to pry more info from Ravi about this new gal in his life when another woman tapped him ruefully on the shoulder.

"Mr. Ravi," she said ironically, or maybe not. "I'm so sorry to interrupt, but I wanted to give you my card. We provided the girls for this evening." Brandishing a card—it read, Two Solitudes Modelling Agency—she added, "We specialize in French- and English-speaking models. And it would be wonderful if you could give us a mention."

As she held his attention for a few minutes, Rory was seized by a bulbously lipped dentist, originally from Côte d'Ivoire. "Champagne isn't very good for your teeth," he was saying, taking an enthusiastic swig. "It's all the acidity. But I don't care!"

So went the party. Waves upon waves. Circles within circles. Eventually, after all the necessary photo-ops had been taken of *Daily Show* correspondents with flutes, and Kathy Griffin had finished pouring a glass all over Chelsea Handler—a spat staged for both of their respective TV shows, of course—Ravi once again assembled with Rory and Leeza. "I think I've had my bubble's worth," he said.

"I want to go out! Montreal is just getting up!" returned the younger lass. Rory said nothing, wisely.

"Feel free, Leeza. But don't stay too, too late. We have to get back to Toronto tomorrow." He gave Rory a wink as he said this.

"That's great. Jason Kevins wants me to go to Time Supper Club with him," she said, pointing to the tamarind-toned comic du jour standing off in the corner. "I'm so into his ethnic humour!"

"Don't do anything I would do!" said Ravi, giving Rory a follow-up wink.

Slipping into a cab, he and the missus then split. Setting out for his hotel, they passed the church where Céline Dion took René Angélil to be her lawfully wedded Svengali and not far from where, come to think of it, Cirque du Soleil founder Guy Laliberté once busked on the street. Into the hotel. Up the elevator. And off with the clothes.

"You wanna know something?" said Rory, coming up sometime later from underneath the sheets.

"That you get into a particularly jolly mood after you've spent some time at a champagne launch targeted at the 'comedic community'?" suggested Ravi.

"Well, that. But what I was going to say is that even though you drive me nuts, I do quite enjoy our little trysts . . ."

"Our non-extramarital affairs . . . ?"

"If nothing else, it does put the sizzle in our marriage."

"You do remember, don't you, what Oscar Wilde said about marriage in *The Importance of Being Earnest*?" Ravi asked her. "'The very essence of romance is uncertainty . . . '" he went on to quote. "'If I ever get married, I'll certainly try to forget the fact.'"

"Oh, Ravi. You know hot and bothered I get when you start quoting Wilde."

"Oh, I know. But don't you worry. One day, we won't have to do this."

Rory looked at Ravi, and Ravi averted his gaze. Then—he had a feeling it was coming—she pointedly asked, "So, this Leeza girl. Who the hell is she?"

"Would you believe me if I told you she's my new life coach?"

"No, Ravi, I would not."

Turning toward her, in a manner that implicitly read, in bright Crayon colours, He's Just Totally Into You, Ravi looked deep into her eyes and said, "Darling, I'll tell you all about it in the morning. Every last detail."

"You promise?"

"I promise, I promise, I promise."

Then, as he took her into his arms, they dissolved into the blinding white light of their intertwine.

9

Plot Thickening with Gyllenhaal

All things considered, writing a gossip column *was* a lot like doing stand-up. At least when it came to the concept of consistency, as described by Steve Martin in *Born Standing Up,* a book Ravi had been reading lately. The legendary jester (of brows low and high) learned a lesson very early on, and it was this: "It was easy to be great." That is to say, "Every entertainer has a night when everything is clicking. These nights are accidental and statistical: Like lucky cards in poker, you can count on them occurring over time."

"What was hard was to be *good,*" Martin went on in the memoir. "Consistently good, night after night, no matter what the abominable circumstances."

Thus it was in his racket, Ravi had quickly apprehended. It wasn't so much about the big scoops. They came, they went. It was more about being in the zone, so to speak. And though a great deal of it was, yes, about serendipity, it was, more urgently, a matter of courting serendipity, or creating the right climate conditions for serendipity.

He had once tried to describe this to a kindred spirit in London who had aptly come back and distilled it to Ravi in the following way: "Actually, it's less about being at the right place at the right time than it is about being at the *wrong* place at the right time."

One night, shortly after their scenery-chewiness in Montreal, the journalist and Leeza were having dinner at Sotto Sotto on Avenue Road when the wrong and the right clanged just so.

"I think I'm going to have the spaghetti bolognese, but I'm asking the waiter to hold the spaghetti," announced Leeza as they waited for someone to take their orders. Before Ravi could get around to giving her his best circumspect stare, she exclaimed, "I'm joking, mister! I'm joking! Not eating carbs is so 2004."

"You look nice," he told her instead, taking in Leeza's retro get-up of mossy green twinset and pearls, with a coif like a 1930s American ingénue. She had the air of a young, Edwardian man-trap keen for a British titleholder to come along and save her ass.

"Have you heard from Mr. Darcy lately?" she asked suddenly.

"I haven't for a bit," said Ravi, stumbling a little because he wasn't sure how much dear Leeza knew about Mr. Darcy and how much she knew that he knew. "I guess we're stuck together for a while longer," he managed as a waiter filled his glass.

"I don't mind," she said quietly, her eyes like comets. "It's actually nice getting out of Hollywood. It's such a rat race."

"Yes, it must be hard being an almost-starlet," he said, trying to commiserate.

"Maybe once Mr. Darcy has figured out a way to kill off Keira Knightley, Natalie Portman, and Anne Hathaway, I'll have a chance."

"Hopefully, he'll get to Miley Cyrus/Hannah Montana while he's at it," rejoined Ravi, playing along.

"Oh, and the Olsen Twins. Both of those twins are just going to have to go."

They both exchanged faux-conspiratorial guffaws at that one and were then interrupted by their waiter.

After their orders had been taken and their overly congenial waiter had gone to do their bidding, there was a wedge of silence, and Ravi took the opportunity to look around while pretending not to look around. Sotto Sotto was a mainstay of the city's feudal classes—a wholly subterranean eatery that drew people night after night, with its moodily lit, Vermeer colouring making all those people better-looking than they really were. It was also where—unusual for this city—paparazzi more often than not stationed themselves, as there was so much in-and-out celebrity traffic. On one night, it could be Justin Timberlake; on another, Sienna Miller or Antonio Banderas. (Both *eTalk* and *Entertainment Tonight Canada*—the two rival showbiz shows—were long rumoured to have secret cameras outfitted in the flower boxes out front.)

At one table, he noticed, there was a hornets' nest of hockey wives, women whose status derived from their husbands playing the almighty national sport. Cheesy, cheesy, like Gouda.

Next to them, as serendipity would have it and as Leeza pointed out, was one Sean Avery—"the most hated man in hockey," as he was called. Known for his hotheadedness and extreme-starlet dating (including one of the Olsens, Ravi forgot which), the Canadian puckmeister was also an unlikely fashion whore (having once interned at *Vogue* during the off-season) and, moreover, a testament to the state Ozzy Osbourne had once clarified: "You don't accidentally become an asshole. It takes a bit of work." At this precise point, the industrious Avery was ordering seconds.

At the back, Ravi couldn't help but detect a distinctly Unabomber-like, bearded Michael Cohl, the showbiz maharishi who was best known for managing the Stones and who was responsible for the quasi-regular invasion of the city by Mick Jagger et al., since the band used Toronto as their rehearsal headquarters. (Alas, no Mick tonight, although there did seem to be an intriguing, Jagger-worthy curtain drawn around the extra-important cove located at the rear.)

At yet another table reigned the much-married and often-face-refreshed home décor deity Reva Linds. And matching her in the ambition department, just one or two candleholders away, was the TV newswoman who he knew was fifty-something but looked like she was going on fifteen. The one who maintained a daily regime that included an hour of Olympic-level Ashtanga yoga and an hour of aerobics, twice-weekly hits of Pilates and chemical peels, but whose hands, as always, gave away the true ravages of time.

Here, as she held up her menu, he could see the topography of age-appropriate veins.

Somewhere between the starters and their skedaddle, the waiter reappeared, bearing not just freshly ground pepper, but an agenda.

"Is everything to your liking?" he asked.

"Fine," said Leeza.

"Thank you," said Ravi.

"I don't mean to disturb and I . . ."

Now the server—who was the kind of chap who appeared to know the names of all his cheeses, and looked as though he took a lot of catnaps—stopped to put his finger on his chin.

"It's just that . . . our sous-chef," he continued.

"Your sous-chef?" prompted Ravi.

"Your sous-chef," rehashed Leeza.

"Our sous-chef . . . well, he's very talented, and . . ."

"Yes?"

The server assumed a crouching position near their table and reverted to a *sotto voce* voice. *Sotto voce,* that is, at Sotto Sotto.

"Our sous-chef," he began again quickly, "he is a rising star. A genius. An artist. He doesn't have the profile because . . . well, he's just a sous-chef. But we all think he's going to be big, and, well, it doesn't hurt that he's very, very good-looking."

The crouching server with the finger on his chin took the opportunity to wink wickedly at Ravi.

"I mean, his pecs are almost as good as his sauces," he extolled, winking again at Ravi and continuing along. "Liv Tyler was here—when she was in town doing that *Hulk* movie—and she caught a glimpse of him, and she said he was good enough to eat."

Leeza, who had continued eating her carbs like a good girl throughout this entire interval, emitted the smallest of giggles.

"Anyhow—I'm really sorry to interrupt, and take up so much time—but I'm his biggest booster in the restaurant, and he's just so talented and, well, we wanted to know when you were planning to do your next eligible list . . . and if you would consider putting him on it."

The voluble waiter was referring to the ranking that Ravi undertook, year in and year out, of single, dateable men and women. It was called the "Foxy Forty," and from its very inception in the *National Mirror* many years ago, it had been a sensation.

He continued, "The thing is, he'd really like to know exactly when the next list is due to come out, 'cause, well, he needs to break up with his fiancée before then."

Ravi, naturally, had heard it all before. "Yes, with a fiancée, he wouldn't quite qualify."

The server, who was presently doing a swell job of ignoring the nearby table of wine-refill-needing hockey wives, elaborated, "She's a really nice girl. Really sweet. But this would just be so good for his profile. Actually, they talked about it, and his fiancée is all in favour of it. They can always get back together after the list comes out, after all."

With this, he got up, while the adjoining gang of seething sports spouses stiffened their poses, all together now, and looked about ready to beat him with a puck.

"Ravi, I mean, sir, he's back there now. If I could just introduce you to him. Just for a second," he said with a vaguely apologetic glance at Leeza.

Before he could go on, Ravi was up from his seat and fluttering toward the kitchen. For one, he simply wanted to put this poor guy out of his misery. For another, he knew there would be trouble if the hockey wives didn't get their Pinot Grigio relatively soon. Thirdly, at this point in the game, he knew this much was true: keep your friends close and your waiters even closer.

Truly, they were beyond valuable to the professional gossipist.

Moving into the kitchen, which was tiny, tiny, tiny and incongruous, really, with the amount of cooking that got done every night, Ravi exchanged greetings with the Jamie Oliver–aspirant. His looks measured up, but before he had a chance to discuss his sauces, something happened that caused quite the clamour.

It was along the lines of what Leo Braudy described so well in his book *The Frenzy of Renown:* that "spiritual glow conveyed by being recognized." The something that "means finally not having to say who you are."

It was—ta-dah!—Jake Gyllenhaal.

Deeply V-necked, pleasantly broad-shouldered, and with that paralyzing dopey smile, he turned up solo, like one of those bit partridges who'd mixed up the time he was supposed to appear in a junior high production of the Twelve Days of Christmas. His baby-blue vee, by the way, looked comfortable but meticulous, as did the black tee underneath the sweater and his near-pristine dark jeans. All very back-to-school clean, under the hard, harsh, unforgiving stovekeeper's light, Ravi thought. The only thing casting a shadow? Jake's ten-o'clock facial buzz. "Mama would like a picture," claimed one of the maybe five men, besides Ravi, in the room.

"Mama"—an ineffable local legend and Sotto Sotto's sorceress *sine qua non*—only spoke the language of food and, well, Italian. And she was dying for a pic. And before Ravi could even mutter, "So, Jake, what brings you here?" this became Agenda Item Number One. Everyone had promptly forgotten all about the sous-chef and his career aspirations.

A shuffle happened, and some others manifested, and the rapt and well-seasoned matriarch was suddenly having her close-up with the man who famously had trouble quitting in *Brokeback Mountain.*

Did Mama see that movie? Or any one of the actor's movies? One couldn't help but wonder. Was Mama a Gyllenhaal-ic? "Actually," whispered one of the other waiters, "Mama has no idea what a Gyllenhaal is. She just likes the idea of having her picture taken with famous people."

Well, of course. Ravi had come across many people like that.

Jake, meanwhile, gave them all a close-up of his singularly sporty-brainy-emo brand of Hollywood—the sort of celebrity who can competitive bike ride, complete crosswords, and get teary-eyed c/o Keats. The night was almost done, and he, polite to the end, thanked everyone and raved, appropriately, about Mama's lasagna.

He, Ravi quickly surmised, had been the one behind the mystery curtain in the dining room. No doubt in town to promote one of his movies. And waiting in the alley behind the restaurant? A dark, mean SUV, ready to get the actor through the back door and escape the growing pulp of paps who were standing out in front. (Only later did Ravi learn that inside the vehicle, ready to pick up Jake and frustrate the cameras, was his good friend Reese Witherspoon. She'd been at a Japanese spot not far away, having her sushi and eating it too. A stagey cross-purposes sighting that gave Ravi an opportunity, in a column yet to be written, to strike with lines such as "Whither Jake?" and "Shall never the twain meet between the wasabi and the lasagna?")

After they'd all seen Mr. Brokeback off, and after our star reporter had solemnly promised to put the ambitious sous-chef in his "Foxy Forty" list (just as soon as the sous-chef broke it off with the love of his life, of course), Mama packed Ravi some of her secret-recipe chili sauce.

Considering that he still had three parties to go to after dinner, he wasn't sure if he wanted to be weighed down by condiments. But, remembering he had the car and driver that night (he'd plugged Cadillac in a column recently), and knowing that it would be rude to decline anything from Mama, Ravi didn't have it in him to say no.

So, he took the chili sauce.

"Was he nice?" asked Leeza upon Ravi returning to their table.

"Oh, yes. Very nice," he said, playing along.

"What's that?" she asked, pointing to the ruby-red thickness caught in a bottle.

"Oh, just some hot chili sauce I picked up," he sighed. "By the way, did I tell you that I ran into . . ."

"Leeza, my child, could I interest you at all in a possible calling of the night?"

That was Ravi, several hard-working hours later, deep in the entrails of a club called D-Loft down near Wellington after a stop at Dooyn on Queen, and a stop before that at And/Or. He and the kid had swept in for the launch of the latest Motorola mobile phone, which, if you didn't know any better, was like any sweaty dance-a-thon except for the DJ behind the booth who had been flown in special from New York. Like many a celebrity DJ in the current epoch, he came from the very highest of echelons, and, in this case, contrary to his deceptive beach-bum bearing, was the heir to a profitable, very profitable, planet-spanning salad bar chain.

"But he's playing the 'Single Ladies' song—and he's mixing it with 'Tiny Dancer'!" Leeza countered, her stunt chignon looking more than a little worn out by this time in the morning.

"I know, I know. But Leeza, my child, I'm just trying really hard to make my life a little less Bret Easton Ellis right now and would very much like to get at least a few hours' sleep."

"Did you know that someone spilled a drink on me—and they said sorry and everything!" Leeza rolled on, clearly not listening. "People in Canada are *so* nice!

"Holy Maple Leaf!" she suddenly exclaimed. "There's that judge from *So You Think You Can Dance Canada*!"

Her parting words, as she flew from their banquette in the general direction of the TV adjudicator's direction, were these: "I met him earlier, and he said all I need to do is get citizenship here and he'll make me the winner."

Ravi inhaled deeply and, exasperated, looked around. Was

that, could it be, in the distance? Nah. False alarm. No Gyllenhaal second helpings tonight. No hot, up-and-coming sous-chefs either. He did see a woman who looked like local neo-hippie songbird Feist but could only really be Feist if Feist were Asian.

Bored, and feeling just a little *Groundhog Day*-ish (clearly, Ravi had been on too many banquettes in too many clubs in too many cities), he noticed that Leeza, in all her *So You Think You Can Dance Canada* mania, had dropped her cranberry-coloured Sergio Rossi clutch on the floor. It was wide open.

Scooping it up, he noticed that some mints had fallen out. And also a piece of paper . . . no, actually a photograph. He looked a little closer.

Well, that's weird, went Ravi's inner voice.

The snap was of the world's most celebrated twins, Mary-Kate and Ashley Olsen. And over their pouty, party-perfect little mouths, someone, very clearly, very pointedly, had taken the time to draw with evil Magic Marker. There lay two hers-and-hers moustaches.

10

Wombmates

The next day, as fate and capricious plotting would have it, Ravi was summoned to discuss the nature of celebrity twins for one of his quasi-regular sound-offs on TV.

Or, as the producer who called him much too early in the morning had sputtered, making like she was calling from Sound-Bite ICU: "We're reeeally desperate. Need someone right away to come in and give us some fun bites on famous twins. For a special that we're doing on twins. We'll give you a stipend, of course."

"Sure thing," said Ravi, thinking a) what a funny word *stipend* is and b) how much easier it was to talk about celebrities than about himself. (For, as gifted as Ravi was at receiving other people's stories, he wasn't much of a confessionist. He liked to keep his own counsel.)

And now, while making his way across town to the destined studio not long after the phone call, his mind rested on those two-for-one American ex-first daughters, Jenna and Barbara

Bush. He also set up the verbal vomiting he might very well do about that married-up pretty boy Ashton Kutcher, who had a little-known twin, and Alanis Morissette, who, not so ironically, had one too. Of course, the whole time, he couldn't stop thinking about Mary-Kate and Ashley, the Olsens being to twins what Sting was to Tantra, and what Orphan Annie was to tomorrow. The greatest girl-ambassadors ever for twinship, to put it mildly. The pixie patron saints of wombmates.

He hadn't said anything to Leeza last night/this morning about coming across that rather odd picture of the two famous sisters—stiff, black upper lips and all—in her purse, but thought he just might at an opportune time. No doubt, she was going to be sleeping in late today. By the time he arrived at the studio for his mid-morning bark-fest, he felt in rant-fighting shape, having popped some constitution-strengthening Emergen-C in the cab, swilled back some de rigueur Vitamin Water for backup, plus dabbed some Kiehl's Facial Fuel on his face (a very good pre-rant pick-me-up, he'd discovered over the years).

"I'm so grateful you were able to make it," said the sputtering woman with the show, taking him up the elevator at the network.

"Any time," he replied, showing some teeth. It was a smile that acknowledged that aside from the never-not-useful promise of a "stipend," Ravi never really gave up an opportunity to opine on television because as a print journalist he knew just how essential it was. After all, working in newspapers, at this juncture in the history of the world, was not unlike being adept at oil painting, or going daily dog-sledding, or knowing Braille.

It was a boutique business, fetishistic, perhaps even a throwback. Though most of the television and Internet headlines still flowed from print—true even to this day, Ravi always noticed—you were d-e-a-d if you weren't on television yourself, and so he did his share of it. It was the thing that marketing peeps called "synergy," and although he didn't like the word, he was certainly not above employing it. Alas, over the years he'd given himself over to the cameras to discuss, with varying degrees of gusto, subjects that ran the following gamut:

"Air Kisses: In or Out?"

"Man-Bangs: Discuss"

"The Ten Greatest On-Again Off-Again On-Again-Again Celebrity Relationships of All Time."

Eventually arriving at this particular TV show bastion—primary-coloured but surprisingly quiet—he found himself behind walls that hummed with the tedium that comes with a newsroom from which both seismic and breathless pronouncements flow daily on matters of showbiz. Moving through a series of dinky rooms that, somehow, courtesy of the magic of TV, appeared like something out of the Playboy Mansion when seen on the small screen, he also discerned the distinct white noise of frustration that emerges naturally from an office full of producer types who grew up wanting to be on TV but for some reason or another had found themselves off-, not on-, camera.

"Here's Shaye," said his producer-host, with the tiniest bit of edge, delivering him to the defiantly on-camera woman waiting to interview him.

Shaye greeted garrulously. Shaye, it should be noted, was

like a Bratz doll come to life and, like most TV personalities, reminded Ravi of a real estate agent, all ready to up-talk a sitting room or a certain walk-in-closet during a weekend open house. Well versed in the Styrofoam language of entertainment television, her lips pursed photogenically, Shaye was dressed, on this particular day, in a knife-sharp jacket and fluted, this-season skirt.

"So, twins," she said to him, splitting the difference between a statement and a question.

"Twins," he returned in a perfect deadpan. If he had a sombrero, he would have tipped it.

A few minutes later, after a spidery microphone had been attached to the inside of his lapel and a little light powder was flecked on his face ("You don't need much with your complexion," marvelled the makeup person), Ravi settled into a nice puffy couch with Shaye.

Lights, camera, conjecture!

"So, twins," began Shaye, parroting her off-camera voice. "Ce-le-be-ri-ty twins."

Knowing that it helps, in these circumstances, to be a little hyperbolic, a lot reductive, and clever to a fault, Ravi pounced.

"You want sibling envy? I'll give you sibling envy! Try being Giselle's twin. Giselle's five-minutes-older fraternal twin! That's right! Burning Brazilian hot, oh my god, babelicious-bodied Giselle has a twin. And not only is she not an international top model with a *Forbes* rating like her sis, but her name says it all. She's Patricia. Just Patricia. Looks like Giselle got the exotic name—and the gazillions! Last I heard, Patricia was an admin assistant back at home in São Paolo. Now that's sibling envy you can take to the bank!"

This last bit, the part about the admin assistant, he had heard somewhere but wasn't entirely sure that it was true. But it sounded good, didn't it?

"Okay, who else do you have for us?" prodded his TV interrogator, giving him the look that TV interrogators give when they want their subject to speak in fewer-second clips.

"Jerry Hall, Mick's ex? She's got a twin! Gorgeous Isabella Rossellini? She's a two-for-one! Action star Vin Diesel? Twin, twin, twin! Apparently—ha!—his twin doesn't work out as much! Abs of Jell-O, not of steel!"

"Let's talk Canadian twins now," said Shaye, keeping things going.

Yes, let's, Ravi said to himself. Out loud, he projected, "Canadians, as you know, have a long and distinguished history in the area of twins. Our own Kiefer Sutherland, for instance, has a twin sister, Rachel, living right here in Toronto. There is also television star Jill Hennessey, and her darling twin, Jacqueline, also living here. Shawn Ashmore—Iceman from the *X-Men* movies—and his mirror image, also an actor, Aaron! Our jazzy Canadian Diana Krall and her bespectacled Brit, Elvis Costello? They're parents of two. Twins, of course. Oh, and there are those all-Canadian Felliniesque twins Dean and Dan, the designers behind the label Dsquared^2. Can't get any more twin than that, now can you?"

"Can you tell us, just a little, about Alanis's twin brother?" said Shaye, licking her photogenic lips just so and framing her words as if she was Christiane Amanpour posing a question to some mullah about the Taliban.

"Well," Ravi dove in. "His name is Wade. Born twelve minutes earlier than that Jagged Little Pill. Wade, my sources tell me, is a yoga instructor on the West Coast, and some time ago he put out an album of his own—of yoga chants."

"Really?"

"Yes. And here's a little something interesting: Alanis, as you know, was once engaged to the well-muscled Ryan Reynolds, a fellow Canadian. After they broke up, he got involved with and eventually married actress Scarlett Johansson, who—get this?—has a twin. His name is Hunter!"

"Really?"

"Now, isn't that ironic?" Sometimes, Ravi just couldn't resist.

Pausing gallantly, he went on, "Indeed. Some men are breast men, others are leg men. Ryan Reynolds, it appears, is a twin man."

A big bear-hug of quiet enveloped Shaye and Ravi. She widened the slits of her eyes, straightened her fluted, this-season skirt, and picked things up with this: "Now, we can't talk about twins without talking about Mary-Kate and Ashley, of course. Thoughts?"

"A long, long time ago," he began, thinking quickly, "in a time before *Dr. Phil,* or *The Hills,* or *The Inconvenient Truth,* there was a show called *Full House.* The Olsen Twins, currently worth somewhere in the upwards of a hundred million dollars, began playing a character named Michelle Tanner. Both sisters played her, in compliance with child labour laws."

"Really?"

"Oh, yes. For the first year, it's been said, Ashley would cry a lot while on-set, so Mary-Kate had more screen time. And because the producers did not want people to know that Michelle was played by twins, the sisters were credited together on the show as Mary-Kate Ashley Olsen. Eventually, they were credited as separate people."

"Well, you certainly learn something every day," she expertly trotted out. And, then, with a flourish: "Last but not least, Ravi, can we talk about twins of the future?"

"Sure! As many close watchers of the hotter-than-ever double-fertilization craze know, Julia Roberts was right on the vanguard when she birthed both Hazel and Phinnaeus back in 2004. Others followed suit. Jennifer Lopez, Marcia Cross, Lisa Marie Presley, Ricky Martin, *younameit!* In 2008, of course, it all reached its highest apex when Brad and Angelina became the parents of the goldenest twins of all, two gorgeous babies named Knox Leon and Vivienne Marcheline."

"Thank you so much for coming in, Ravi."

And that was what they called a wrap.

11

Social Kabuki

Slightly worn out, Ravi shuffled out onto the street. It was a sunny day but not exactly hot, so Ravi stopped to put on his sunglasses and pull up his collar in one of those insouciantly hot-cold moves. He started to walk, partly because he loved nothing more than a crisp day and partly to help keep up with the adrenalin that comes after a heavy pundit workout. Then, catching himself in the reflection of a nearby restaurant—a Jamaican/Thai place, it looked like, part of a glorious nod to Canada's multicultural makeup—he thought that the up-collar thing looked just a little too much like he was trying to be James Spader in one of those 1980s movies when James Spader was skinny, so he turned the collar down.

A streetcar vibrated past him. Which is when a spooky, disembodied tingle went through his body. It was his phone, which he'd put on vibrate during the interview.

"Hi. Aren't you going to that party?" said the man who kept tabs sparingly on the other end.

It took a minute to realize that this was Mr. Darcy, but Ravi had no idea what party he was talking about. In fact, Ravi thought it was rude not to specify. Asking him if he was going to a party was like asking James Taylor if he was going to perchance sing a ballad, or Rush Limbaugh if he had something he maybe wanted to get off his chest.

But he bit. "What party?"

"That party for that British vacuum inventor! You have to be there now, I do believe."

"It's a reception actually, not a party," he corrected Mr. Darcy, remembering, indeed, that there was an in-store event he was supposed to be at just about now. He wasn't, though, going to give the mysterious man the satisfaction of asking him how he knew Ravi's schedule better than Ravi did because he knew that he'd just get one of those annoyingly mysterious "I have my ways" answers in return.

"I thank you for keeping me on top of my schedule," Ravi went on. "But that isn't why I called you late last night. What I'd like to know, is . . . well, anything further you want to tell me about Leeza Pellegrino? Like what, pray tell, is her thing with the Olsen Twins?"

Was that a slight gasp of air he heard coming from Mr. Darcy? "What?"

"You heard me, the Olsen Twins."

Just then, his other line went. It was, he could see, a long-distance call from his mom, and in the interest of being an involved and present son, he decided he should take it. The woman always did have a distinct sense of timing.

"Hold on a second. I gotta take this."

"Ravi?" she began in her choppy-charming immigrant brogue. "It's Mummy. My friends, they say you were stirring pot on television last night. Everybody saw you!"

"Excuse me?" He really didn't like the accusatory tone in his mother's voice.

"Stirring pot! You stirring. And there was a pot!" she said, not wasting any time in breaking out in actual sobs. "It's so shameful."

"But, Mummy, that was a repeat!" he blurted out, protesting. He was now approaching the cacophonous ticks of Chinatown on his walk and had to block one ear to adequately hear his mother's wails.

Trying a more conciliatory tone, and trying not to get too generation gap in a *Bend It Like Beckham* sort of way with his mother, as he passed by some hanging upside-down fish on Spadina Avenue, he tried, "I'm not a cook. It was a television show on the Food Network, and I was a special guest that day. A guest! We taped it eons ago, Mummy, and I was helping to make the sauce."

"But what will people think?" she struck back as melodramatically as an Indian mother can get, with a fresh outpour of snobs. "That my son is a cook! No son of my mine will be a cook! Cooking like a servant on television, for everybody to see!"

Ravi struck back: "I was a special guest. It's a good thing. They only ask important or quasi-famous people to be guests, and they asked me! I promise you, I'm not really cooking!"

He wanted to tell his stuck-in-her-ways mom that in the Age of Foodies, chefs were big celebrities now, even brands, and there was no shame to be had from cooking, but he knew that this would take more than one phone conversation to get through. Plus, he didn't want to push his luck, as it had only been a year since he broke the news that her Good Indian Son was not a doctor, and not ever going to be one either, and that this writing thing might indeed be for keeps.

"Don't stir pots no more!" she cried out to him, blowing her nose into the phone. "Promise me! No pots! No pots!"

"I promise, Mummy," he said, not exactly lying and not actually pointing out that all he did via his column was stir pots. "But I really have to go. I have another call right now." Click.

"Mr. Darcy?" he asked, switching lines as he passed a shop bearing shiny, big baskets full of papayas out front. A blast of wind, complicit with autumn, hit both them and him.

"I was about to lose hope."

"Sorry, it was . . ."

"Ravi, I can't discuss this now, but I advise you not to ask Leeza anything about the Twins Olsen until we've had a chance to talk properly." He paused. "Which we can do in a couple of days. Can you promise me that?"

Not impervious to the sneaky flowing from Mr. Darcy's voice, he decided to grow a backbone right there in Chinatown, standing as he was now in front of a well-trod dumpling dive called Swatow. "Now, listen here, what are you not telling me? What is it you really want? I've been very patient, waiting for you to give me further instructions, as you promised from the start. This plot is seriously moving slower than *The Curious Case of Benjamin Button*!"

"I don't—"

"Don't don't me! I've been very good at playing along, and I still don't know any more about this Leeza Pellegrino Operation than I did when we first met! Are you gaslighting me? What's the real story?"

"Ravi, we will talk soon," he said, unrelenting. "You will have one heck of a story when this is over, so just sit tight for a bit longer and continue to entertain and enlighten the lovely Ms. Pellegrino."

"But, I . . ."

"If I know anything, I know how addicted people like yourself can get to your own bylines, so I trust you'll have no qualms about waiting."

This was perhaps the most convincing (and true) thing to come out of the sweater-vested man in a while, but just then, his other line yet again announced itself. What was this? Was his cell phone provider in cahoots with Mr. Darcy?

"Ravi, I'll let you take that," he said as a parting. Click.

"Hello?" he queried, flipping to the latest call.

"Hello, my sugarcube. Are you going to that party?"

It was Rory, his long-lost ball-breaker. Ravi took the opportunity to hop into a cab snailed presently on Spadina, near the favoured dumpling dive. Jumping in and giving the driver a Marlee Matlinesque impression of cab directions, he continued gabbing.

"You were saying?" he asked. "*Party?*"

"I remember you mentioning that vacuum party today, and I was wondering if you were thinking about getting a free vacuum cleaner for me. Well, for us. For a day, when it comes, when we fully share a carpet—and a life—together."

Ravi could take a hint when he heard one. "Rory, Rory Rory, please forgive me. I know I haven't been giving one hundred percent to this relationship, but as you know, a lot of things have suddenly come up. It's this whole Leeza Pellegrino thing, and well, there is also that whole other matter we need to clear up before we can go public with our love." Was his wife tele-seething? Yes, it certainly seemed so.

"So, you're still not in the clear?" she persisted. "You still haven't heard?"

"No, I haven't," he said. "And you know they won't give me the fellowship if they know I'm married . . . to you."

"I'm with you," came her voice, solemnly. "I know it's two years in Paris. I know it's all-paid. I know, I know."

He thought she was going to say, *But what about us?* So before she did, he filled up the fallow silence with this: "I'm doing this for the both of us, Rory. I'll finally be footloose and party-free. And you, I'll be able to give you the adventure of a lifetime. Once we get to Paris, we can take it from there. But first let's just get to Paris."

"And to do that . . . well, they can't know you're not friends with Dorothy. I get it."

"Where are you now, anyways?" he asked, turning things around.

"In London. Still on business. But I'll be back soon, and when I do get back we're going to get to the bottom of this, okay? And I'm also going to help you with this Pellegrino girl situation. I feel you might be over your head with this Princess Protection Program."

"Yes, Rory."

"No, seriously."

"Yes, Rory."

"Now, say it. Say the thing you told me when we first met."

Ravi remembered. How could he not? It had been at one of those soul-sapping soirees, and she'd been pithy, salty, and vividly in the present. There, they had bonded promptly over a discussion of their favourite words in the English language. His, he'd told her, was *gig*. Hers, she'd shared, was *purée*. Both of them felt, quite emphatically, that *divorcee* was one of the funniest words of all. And, oh, how she had made him laugh! Laugh not in an overly genteel we're-at-party-and-let's-hee-because-we're-social-organisms-and-because-laughing-is-only-the-right-thing-to-do, but laugh in a tremendous, colossal, right-from-the-tummy kind of whoop. And she'd kept him laughing, hers like a saucy, throaty cackle that bubbles up from deep inside and erupts with throw-your-head-back glee. He'd laughed since the day they'd met, and certainly since the day that they'd rather impulsively wed. Even though their relationship was complicated—his need for secrecy, her international banking job, his inability to focus—their easy camaraderie had never once been polluted.

"Say it!" she pressed on now, with an added piquancy in her voice. "Please."

"Okay." Pause. "Love means never having to say you're Rory."

"That's it, tiger," she said, showing once again she was the kind of woman who got off on aphorisms, and even more on a bad pun. Neither of them said anything for a bit, letting the romance build, and all Ravi could hear, for at least a minute, was the gabble coming from the taxi dispatcher machine up front.

The middle-of-the-afternoon vacuum party—the one he'd almost forgotten to go to—appeared to be in mid-session when the cab pulled up to the high-end furnishing shop where it was being held. On numerous occasions, more than a few, Ravi had been accused of attending the opening of an envelope, and now, he snickered, he was about to attend the opening of a dust bag. Except for the fact that, here, there was none.

This party, which was actually a product launch disguised as a party, was designed to welcome Sir James Dyson, known the world over for creating the nifty bag-free DC01, a "cleaner that sucks like a sex-crazed limpet," as one newspaper once put it. Hot little Dyson numbers lined up here, near the entrance, like starlets on a red carpet. And lined up to meet Dyson, direct from Britain? A swirl of devotees, some of whom obviously liked the dashing, Q-tipped rock star–inventor type, some who simply got a kick out of talking to anyone who's worth somewhere in the area of $1.5 billion, and yet others still who were just plain technology whores.

"Come, meet," rushed in the PR woman, wasting no time in delivering Ravi to the tall, jolly, and triumphantly thin guest of honour. Showing the gift for compliments that all Brits of his caste have, and his obvious capacity for sucking up, Dyson immediately complimented Ravi on his socks, which today were of a stripy sort.

"Well, when the shoe fits," Ravi said. "Or should I say vacuum nozzle?"

Dyson chuckled. Ravi repaid him with an adjoining compliment. Both exchanged business cards, further ripostes.

This was going well. He could feel it in his party bones. This sort of exchange, after all, was so much easier and less complicated than covering the society circuit, where things were so much more oblique and laden with layers. The inventor here was talking to him because he wanted publicity for his designer appliances, and Ravi was talking to him because he wanted fodder (and possibly a vacuum to call his very own). In the society swirl, by comparison, there was a lot more social Kabuki involved, and it invariably took a lot more translation to figure out why somebody was talking to him, and whether they were talking to him because they wanted to be mentioned by him or talking to him so they wouldn't be mentioned, or be mentioned, yes, but in a non-mention sort of way. It could all be so exacting.

Dyson being to British technology what Kate Moss is to across-the-pond fashion, Ravi stepped up and asked him what he thought of those famous Luddites in his homeland, those particularly tweedy people who revel in not knowing about technology.

"There is a reverse snobbery," he acknowledged about a certain breed of Brit. "They boast about not knowing."

"Or," offered Ravi, "I expect they have people who will turn on the computer for them."

"Exactly, chum." The inventor's eyes wavered and focused anew on a nearby assistant, who eagerly read her boss and brought over a live red one. "Say, have you tried one of our beauties?"

"I'm afraid not. Not much of a domestic." Ravi set his voice light, always light.

"Well, go ahead."

Ravi fingered the bequeathed vacuum, but he was confused. "No carpet here, sir."

"No, no," guffawed Dyson, sounding devout as he did so. "Just slam it!"

"Excuse me?"

"Slam it! I mean it."

"But, I . . ."

"Slam it! Just do it! You have to." He let out a grin. "It's unbreakable. All my vacuums are absolutely, certifiably one hundred percent unbreakable."

Ravi touched the machine before him gingerly, like she was a virgin bride, as the whole room, the whole party, turned toward him. Dyson's grin, already murderous, turned terrifically animated. Others gathered around, some clucking, as if this was Salem and what he had in his hand was a witch that needed barbecuing. "Slam it!" a fellow journalist cried. "Slam it!" rang out several others.

So, Ravi did. Slammed it as hard as he could, slammed it to the great satisfaction of its creator. The machine didn't even get so much as a dent. And, as it was widely noted afterwards, that particular slam did more damage to the wood floor at the furniture shop that it did at all to the virile vacuum.

The Englishman beamed superbly. Then his eyes wandered over to his assistant, who could right way translate what her boss no doubt seemed to be saying: Gift this nice man a vacuum. Now.

"Are you sure you want us to have it?" asked the nice but suspicious woman at the desk.

"Oh, yes," he said, lining the box with the Dyson in it up against a dying potted plant. He was standing now in the lobby of a women's shelter.

"It looks like a good one," said the woman, admiringly.

Ravi nodded. Right after securing another cab, and dragging his new gift with him into the back seat—the vacuum was not only sturdy but incredibly light—he'd told the driver to take him to the nearest shelter that Ravi could think of.

How tired he was—and, to think, it wasn't even 3 o'clock yet. After all that arduous opining on world-famous twins, and the Jake Gyllenhaal meet-and-greet the night before, and the four party stops late into the night after that, and the calls this morning from his wife and his mom, and all that head-hurting stuff about Leeza and Mr. Darcy, and then all the physical activity at the furniture shop party, he couldn't wait to take a nap. Good grief, did people have any idea just how *hard* gossip columnists worked?

But first, oh first, he'd just had to give this brand-spanking-new vacuum to charity. It was the least he could do. If his life was going to be messy, and his line of work less than pure, at least someone deserved to have a clean floor. He knew that Rory wanted a vacuum, but his need for redemption was bigger at this point than his need to wife-please. Besides, if all went well, he would soon be able to buy two vacuums for his beautiful, brilliant Rory. Twenty vacuums, even!

"Please," said Ravi to the woman in the shelter, "take it." And then he walked out.

12

Murder, She Wrote

"Well, hello, Peggy, how are *you*? I just love what you've done with your hair!"

"Julian! Anna! It's been forever! So, Julian, sued anyone good lately?"

"I have to confess I haven't read any of the books nominated tonight. I was too busy shopping for shoes to go with this dress. It was harder than you'd think. Check out these Roger Vivier buckles! Are they *Belle du Jour* or are they *Belle du Jour*?"

"I totally have back-flap photo-envy. He's got such a good author's pic, and mine sucks. I should have had it done in black and white."

"We just got back from Yunnan. It's China's last frontier."

"It's so hot in here, I can hardly breathe."

"I'm so hot I think I'm going to lay an egg."

"Our man Ivory is his own worst enemy. The punishment may not fit the crime, but I predict he's going to get six years in jail. Minimum."

"Tell me I'm wrong, but his poll numbers are limper than Stephen Hawking's cock. There's no way he's gonna win that election."

"Hemingway, you know, spent some time working at the *Toronto Star.*"

"Krystyne! Scott! Were you both at Il Cantinori in New York last Thursday? Or was it last Wednesday? Actually, I forget myself, but I looked across the room during lunch then and I said to myself: I bet you that's Krystyne and Scott!"

"Her prose is nowhere as good as her plotting, but no one can write a murder scene like she can. By the way, are you wearing Ungaro?"

"Adrienne! John! What a sight for sore eyes!"

"Peter! Melanie! How was Montenegro?"

"Is it me, or is it really hot in here?"

The chit-chat rained down on Ravi at the Four Seasons, the pleasantries and the flatteries pelting him at every turn, all the cynicism polished to a very high sheen. It was the night of the Giller Prize, a yearly event that marks the handing out of the most ka-ching award for literature in Canada and never, ever, fails to send the city into invitation panic. Tonight, as he walked into the second-floor reception area—a sub-lobby, really—he noticed all manner of appropriately gowned damsels (some of them pear-shaped), all-grown-up-now horndogs (some of them smarty-panted), and plenty of robo-schmoozers (all relatively well read and ready to let it rip). It was one of those nights when the politicians came out to show that they could be cultural, the culture types turned up to be political, while society (or what was left of it) arrived to strive and try a medley of both.

Not surprising in a crowd such as this, there was no end of erotic punctuation (writers who had been spurned by certain editors), several grass-is-greener hugs (certain klepto publishers wanting to steal away certain writers), and an insurmountable avoiding-of (six degrees of sarcasm, you might call it).

"Wow, some of these literati are pretty super-awesome," noted Leeza, making the voyeuristic march with him on this night.

He'd ended up bringing her after she'd begged and begged and because a) she'd never been to a book awards party before and as she put it, "I'll try anything once" and b) it was, as she reminded him, a rerun of *How I Met Your Mother* that night anyway. For the occasion, his date—always a mistress of disguises—had come dressed as a junior-league Frida Kahlo, minus the unibrow and the polio. She wore a really long, ready-to-be-stepped-on peasant dress and colourful hair ribbons.

"I don't think you can say 'these literati,'" Ravi suddenly chimed in, playing grammar cop. "You might want to try 'some of these literati types are hot.'"

"Good point, Ravi," exclaimed the officious-enough Leeza.

As they approached the vicinity of the bar, he could see the aging outline of the woman best known as the Formidable Authoress—a writer who was an international commodity and, in this room at least, an unequivocal tiger prawn among all the commonplace crustaceans. Today, she had on a home-crocheted macramé toga-type thing with a nice-enough neckline, and her hair was held up by something that looked like a flask. Her latest book—*The Five Horses of the Apocalypse*—had won her too many prizes from too many juries in too many countries. A few years ago, she had called Ravi in an awesome huff, after finding out he was planning to write a little thing about her stripper ex-daughter-in-law. NutraSweetening her words just so, she then tried (unsuccessfully) to dissuade him from writing on this particular subject—a call that, at that point in time, he'd found both ironic and flattering.

"I don't choose my subjects," he heard her now saying to an overly flush sycophant and the sycophant's later-in-life muse. "My subjects choose me."

As usual, the Formidable Authoress did not speak, she *intoned.* To many, she reminded them of that snail-mouthed waiter you'll find in certain posh restaurants who, after you've told him what you'd like to order, finds himself answering back to you, "Excellent choice." The way those two words are strung together, it's clear, oh so clear, that the waiter isn't praising you but, rather, congratulating himself.

Secretly, Ravi really loved the old dame's writing.

"See that somewhat cocoa-coloured famous author with the Marxist beard?" he asked Leeza, pointing toward a particularly cacophonous area of the increasingly sweat-inducing sub-lobby.

"Yesss?" asked Leeza.

"Go talk to him. That's Michael Ondaatje. He wrote *The English Patient.*"

"Omigod! Do you think he can introduce me to Ralph Fiennes?!"

She was gone faster than the champagne in some people's flutes.

Returning to the bar for another glass of bubbly, complete with obligatory Emergen-C sprinkling, he passed a certain gay curmudgeon and then squeezed himself in between a chattering Ed Greenspan and a griping Ed Greenspon. One was a big-time attorney and the other a big-deal journo, and people were forever mixing them up. Even Ravi—whose very job was to put the names to the faces—had some trouble keeping it straight.

Taking in some of the harried air-kissing and florid navel-gazing, he then watched Nadia Knox walk in, dressed in a billowing affair of red. An actress of a certain age, she was most famous for starring in a fast-paced TV series of mild acclaim about ten years ago. She hadn't done much lately—except, for the looks of it, microdermabrasion—but in this room, she was, year after year, the biggest fish, and in a case of classic national self-deprecation, the photographers circled her like she was Britney Spears at a gas station, jostling hard to get a shot. It was, frankly, ridiculous and made more so when a more of-the-moment actress, with gravitas to boot, Sandra Oh, that Canadian champ from *Grey's Anatomy*, walked in not so long after.

Keeping track of his date, he looked across the room, only to find that Leeza, the fake-Frida, had moved on from her tete-à-tete with the Author of a Book Which Had Been Made into an Oscar-Winning Movie and was now firmly entrenched in a conversational threesome with a Captain of Industry and a Media Luminary.

"Who's the Fresh Face?" asked a voice out of nowhere. It was Sam, his editor, doing his best not to be mistaken for the next Cary Grant by drinking a beer straight from the bottle. It was, needless to say, the finest domestic.

"Hey, Sam. She's related to one of the nominees, in from out of town," he lied easily.

"She's a meal. Introduce me."

"She's much too young for you," said Ravi, making sure to avoid eye contact with Sam, so as not to miss anything at the party.

"And she's altogether too female for you," went his editor, handing out a wan smile. Sam went on. "Well, you fuckwit, maybe you ought to introduce her to the richest man in the room then."

Before he could ask who he was talking about, Ravi zeroed in on the Daddy Warbucks of the hour. The richest man in the room also just happened to be the richest man in the country, and also the eleventh or twelfth in the world, come to think of it. You wouldn't know it from his get-up, though. As far as going-out tuxedoes went, his was an incredibly outdated edition. Too rich to care? Possibly. The harem-style pants gave it away. In fact, the tux paired with those scuffed, comfy lace-up shoes reminded him a little of John Cusack's tan slacks and ankle-high sneakers in *Say Anything*. And though the hair screamed early Eagles, Ravi actually found it kind of refreshing and rock 'n' rolling. He looked every bit the rakish heir. Rumour had it that he gave blood once a month; regular blood donation was an excellent way of doing a cleanse among the super-rich. Rumour also had it that he never just used a teabag once, and that he happened to have sperm of steel. In fact, so proficient was he at impregnating the ladies that he could make a mummy out of even the most infertile of them. A woman could be dropped into an active volcano, trapped in a side cave deprived of oxygen and breathing in lava fumes for a month (while pushing fifty), and still his boys would have little problem wrangling great expectations.

"Thank the Lord he's here," said Ravi to Sam. "He just gave me something to write about."

"Why don't we just recycle our headline from last year . . ."

"And the year before that . . ." added Ravi.

"Giller Thriller!" shouted both men at once.

Just as Sam had gone off to fetch another brew, Ravi noticed that the Richest Man in the Room/Country had on his arm that actress-producer-fiancée-muse of his, Caitlin Rockon. She was the latest of wives-to-be. The previous spousal unit had come and gone in a flash, but not without some serious negotiations, because as it had often been said about these Big Money divorces, they tended to be either terribly straightforward because there was a lot of money or very complicated because there was a lot of money.

"Are those Ferragamos that Caitlin has on?" he immediately texted a friend who would know and who happened to be on the other side of the room. He could have easily just walked right over and asked this friend, but she got antsy being spotted talking to him at a party because she feared that everyone would know that she was one of his "sources," even though, truth be told, everybody pretty much knew already.

"Correct," texted back the fashion-conscious pal, just as quickly as he'd expected. "Yes, black and white pumps, slight trim on the side. This season, but not next season, which is what

I would expect from Caitlin Rockon. The coral pout she's got on is c/o a new lipstick by Chanel, allow me to add. By the way: lunch tomorrow?"

Ravi took this opportunity to study this jackpot-hitting blonde specimen-actress some more. As far as rumours about her went, word was she had stopped being a lipstick lesbian only very recently. Her fashion shrubbery on this night consisted of a ballgown—and, oh, this was a ballgown—which projected a kind of Goth-Madonna-in-the-"Frozen"-video-from-her-*Ray-of-Light*-days feel. Besides the fabulous but not fashion-forward Ferragamo pumps, what also stuck out was the stain-removing Tide pen she held tightly in one hand.

With the just-in-case Tide pen, Caitlin wasn't taking chances. Clearly. Which was good, especially on this night, when unbeknownst to all, jeopardy was shuttling fast toward them.

Cavernous and neo-classical, blue and gold and chandeliered. This was the room where they trampled off to next to put dinner down their gullets and be sermonized to. The Pure Joy of Reading was one of the more common themes from the podium. The Corridors Where Literature Takes You was yet another.

"Fiction rocks!" giggled Leeza while diving into the irony-battered fish and chips that was part of the incongruous standard fare at the yearly affair.

"Jian," asked Ravi of the insouciantly moisturized public broadcaster also bequeathed to their table, "would you kindly pass the gravy?"

"'Come not between the dragon and his wrath,'" said a man for no good reason. He was a pundit with a Nabokovian nose and one who charged ten thousand dollars per speaking engagement.

"*King Lear*," he then alerted, not waiting for either Leeza or anyone else to ask where he had pulled out this stupendous quote. His air was the kind that married weariness with vanity.

"Oh, is he related to Queen Latifah?" she asked him, giving Ravi a kick under the table.

The academic quietly fumed. Then—after eating like he was being paid to—he was up from his seat. Nobody who was anybody stayed in their seat at a dinner such as this, after all. There was too much bear-hugging and back-slapping to do, not to mention so much table-hopping between courses that it was akin to speed-reading.

While Ravi got up and did his own obligatory networking—if you can't beat 'em, etc.—he mused on this subject. Somewhere along the road, he had noticed, it became de rigueur to not sit through an entire meal. To some extent, it was part of the wider erosion of manners but seemed particularly poignant in this age of computer addiction and ADD-ism. Even at the best of parties going out was akin to web surfing—and, well, who can help but scroll?

Before him was that woman who was a socialite but preferred to be called a philanthropist, off every which way like a scattering atom. Particularly frenzied, too, was that Edward Greenspon (or was it Greenspan?). Around the table where sat the Richest Man in Canada and his bride-in-waiting stood so many people—all nodding and speaking ponderously—it seemed like a meeting of the College of Cardinals at the Vatican.

Going to a gala—or to a restaurant, for that matter—was always as much about working as it was about eating. You're out to be seen, to be inventoried, to send non-verbal cues to the tribe about your worth. In that sense, the table almost got in the way; the table was, indeed, beside the point. It was a scene that played out at countless dinners on countless nights. For example: when Rachel Zoe—super-thin L.A. stylist to stars like Nicole Richie and Lindsay Lohan—was at a dinner hosted by Tom Ford, the former Gucci wizard, at Wolfgang Puck's steakhouse, Cut, it was reported that the designer became visibly irked when he noticed that Zoe's chair was empty.

"It was rude. She came for drinks and left, even though it was a small, seated dinner," a source ratted out to the *New York Post*'s "Page Six." "She went to another party, then came back for dessert to make it look like she had been there all along. So tacky."

Italian fashion king Valentino has similar thoughts on the subject. Some time ago, he'd bristled to a magazine, "I notice that young ladies in New York tend to move around the room more, oftentimes before the second course has been served. I do not approve of this and believe in staying seated from first course to dessert."

"Good luck, Signor Valentino," muttered Ravi under his breath as he now circled the room. That was as likely as peace coming to the Middle East—or the Alec Baldwin–Kim Basinger clan. From the looks of it, the whole continent, not just New

York, was doomed, and it wasn't just the ladies who were part of the problemo.

On his way back to his table, he happened to pass by a soupy-looking gal slouched against one of the walls. She had a pained feel about her, and appeared aimless and noodle-armed and not so gung-ho. Like a lifelong smoker who'd had her Player's Lights taken away from her rather suddenly. By the looks of it, too, she seemed like someone who might have once been Somebody.

Hmm.

Back at square one, Leeza was reading the issue of *InStyle* she'd brought along in her purse just in case she got bored. "I can't remember, does Halle Berry have a white mother and a black father, or is it a black father and a white mother?" This was her opening gambit upon his return, pointing to a pic in the mag of Halle standing beside Gabriel Aubry, her hot French-Canadian baby daddy.

Before he could say a thing, there was, in living colour, Justin Trudeau, the dashing son of the hottest French Canadian ever, the late, beloved prime minister Pierre Trudeau. Wearing a coat of Teflon and drenched in eau de nepotism, Justin was on stage to glam things up, introduce some of the nominees, and make some opening remarks.

"Single?" whispered Leeza, almost right on cue.

Ravi shook his head and then tried hard to stay awake.

The young Trudeau, so famously born on Christmas Day, started off by introducing the rosy-cheeked senior citizen crowd-pleaser who, some years ago, had founded this award, in memory of his late, well-read wife, in effect installing the Giller Prize as a kind of Taj Mahal to her. Then, the emcee turned to other matters. "It's all in the parable of Pythagoras," Trudeau was saying, in a voice built for flamboyant bed-y-time stories. "There it is written: life is like a festival; just as some come to the festival to compete, some to ply their trade, but the best come as spectators, so in life the slavish men go hunting for fame or gain; the philosophers for truth . . ."

It was then that Ravi, and the rest of the crème de la crème, noticed that the skinny, schleppy, grim-looking woman who'd been hugging the wall just a little while earlier was now in the middle of the room, looking unhappier by the second, and flashing what appeared to be a . . .

"Gun!" intoned the Formidable Authoress.

"She's got a pistol!" reiterated a certain agent who was known for being one.

"Nooo!"

"Oh, heaven!"

"Yikes!"

"Ya Allah!"

"Ahhh!"

"Someone, quick! Get her!"

The ballroom was in auto-bedlam, and there were tantrums aplenty. The armed and kitteny woman inched closer, and then closer still, to the stage. The Gay Curmudgeon took out his rosary, while the Richest Man in Canada mopped some sweat off his brow. One Media Luminary fainted. A certain Captain of Industry screamed just like a girl.

Justin, meanwhile, had gone into de facto ducking-down position behind the podium.

"We're going to die," the big-pay pundit at their table stage-whispered.

"Literally!" Ravi added, not allowing this crisis to get in the way of an obvious play on words. He grabbed the hand of Leeza, who, by now, was holding up her *InStyle* magazine as a make-shift shield.

"Please, everybody stay calm." This from Sandra Oh, who, it was true, only played a doctor on television but who evidently had picked up a thing or two about grace under pressure.

"All you people! You think you're so great, don't you?" leered the gun-toter, having moved into the centre of the room. She was flailing furiously and popping both eyes. All teeth. Jutting jaw.

"All you people with your books and your bylines and your fancy parties."

"Madam, please," tried a left-wing woman who currently had 145,000 Google entries on her name, was having an affair with a personal trainer who regularly came to her house to help her with her laptop-caused shoulder issues, and was now trying very much to go the rational route. "Please do put down the weapon. Did Michael Moore and his *Bowling for Columbine* teach you nothing? We have very strict gun laws in this country. You can't do this!"

"Just watch me," said the gun-toter with a bludgeoning stare, turning her head now in the direction of the mousy Trudeau. "You all think you're so great," she followed up with a snort, beginning to sob in this, a melodrama of her own making. "Why isn't it me? Why isn't it ever me!" Clearly, somewhere along the line, she'd attended the *Days of Our Lives* Advanced Academy of Overacting.

"My goodness. That's Hana Mizoko!" the pundit suddenly said, nudging nosily at everyone around him. "It's her! I almost didn't recognize her. Always wondered what happened to her."

Various voices added to the ripple. "It's Hana! It's Hana!"

Hana Mizoko, Ravi now remembered, was a writer who had once held the town in thrall. A fame-junkie of the highest degree, she'd arrived from New Brunswick via a vague degree in Something Studies, not taking long to land a column that nicely covered the bases of work, sex, and big-city life. The column was widely touted for its gameful consideration of hip fashion, surreal nightclubs, and disaffected young people, but it was no secret that her subject was the ins-and-outs of herself. She being she, Hana even appeared at a party dressed up like a female dog, showing, shrewdly, her precise ability to give her detractors what they wanted. After getting pregnant—accidentally on purpose—she quickly pumped out several books, including one entitled *Dior in Headlights,* a modern-day update on *Memoirs of a Geisha.* But she'd only succeeded in flaming out instead of fanning faster, increasingly frustrated by the fact that her particular femme fataleness was waning, and packed full of self-loathing about her lost singleton years.

So, now she stood, with her stabbing glance and her once-long, lustrous locks reworked into a Camilla Parker Bowles cut.

"You never liked me," the chaos-causer was saying, flying from table to table, heaving like a contestant on *The Biggest*

Loser. "Never nominated me for anything!" She waved her gun. In response, most made like Madame Tussauds. "My books were too hipster, too downtown-geisha, weren't they? Too many apple martinis! Too much sex, you said! My books aren't coming-of-age stories set in the prairies, right? Well, screw you, literati! Screw all of you!"

Leeza, who was now managing the mean feat of looking fashionably bored but deeply perturbed all at the same, turned to Ravi for some reassurance. He did her the favour, uncrossing his arms in an attempt to avoid telegraphing any bad body language. But privately he fretted. This was scary stuff. Scarier than the time that Michael Jackson married Lisa Marie Presley. Scarier than the possibility of sharing a pied-á-terre in Burma with Mike Tyson.

Rising across the room was the Formidable Authoress, who clearly looked like she'd had enough and was now going to use her considerable gravitas to stop this madwoman cold.

"Ms. Mizoko," she intoned. "This nonsense must cease this minute."

Bam! The Miz interrupted her with a shot in the air. And then—bam!—another. Ravi and his date, the faux-Frida, dived underneath their table, as did so many others in the room.

"I can't die," Leeza said as they sat shrouded in a tablecloth and as the noise around them rose to hooligan levels. Her eyes were huge. "I just can't! I haven't even won an Oscar yet."

"Or even an MTV Award for Best Kiss," he reminded her.

"Ravi?" she asked.

"Yes?"

"If I don't make it, I want people to know . . . I want people to know the truth."

"The truth?"

"I have a confession." With that, Leeza paused. Shots continued, screams sounded, but Ravi felt that the real drama was happening under his table.

"It's about the Olsen Twins."

"Okay."

"I'm not who you think I am."

"Can you kindly get on with it, Leeza? We're sort of in a holdup situation here."

Out there, somewhere, there was the muffled sound of cops arriving. The pop of another gunshot. Perspiration spurting. More clatter, more screams.

Leeza took Ravi's hand, adjusted the ribbons on her hair, and then, emoting beautifully underneath the tablecloth, she said, "You should know. I am the third Olsen. I am the Olsen Triplet."

13

Jihad Bell Rock!

It happened like that, just that fast.

Often, these things do. A string of events. One fork in the road, or four, taken or not. Messing up life's map altogether. If Pam Anderson had not shown up at that B.C. Lions football game in Vancouver, and that JumboTron had not caught her in her Labatt's tee, and the crowd had not cheered, and Labatt had not then offered her a modelling deal, and she had not gone on to do *Playboy* and *Baywatch,* would she and her all-Canadian physique have ended up in our pop consciousness forever more? If Elizabeth Hurley had not been Hugh Grant's girlfriend in 1994, and she hadn't shown up at the London premiere of *Four Weddings and a Funeral,* and she hadn't chosen to wear that famously safety-pinned Versace dress, would she really have gone on to live that *HELLO!*-heaving existence that she does?

And so it was that night in Toronto at that literary shindig. If Leeza Pellegrino hadn't decided to go with Ravi to the event, all folked out in her Frida, and Hana Mizoko hadn't decided to lose it on that particular night, she wouldn't have ended up blowing her cover in the way that she had underneath that tablecloth, amid all that screw-tightening tension. "I am the third Olsen."

Olsen. Triplet.

Ravi had heard her; he just hadn't quite understood. But was it any time to go begging for clarifications? Instead, he'd just gestured a strong feeling of gravity, and because he'd always been taught that it's only polite, when receiving a confession, to make a polite confession of one's own, he'd spilled.

"Well, that's nothing," he'd heard himself say as the sounds of mayhem and gunfire raged. "I've been keeping a secret too. I actually can't stand champagne."

"What?" burst out Leeza.

"It's true. I'm a professional social butterfly, and I really hate champagne. I squirm every time someone hands me a glass. And I can't not drink bubbly. No, darling, not in my line of work."

The confession had not had much time to bloom because shortly after that, the cops had indeed arrived, and Hana Mizoko, the haywire hack, was carted away in handcuffs. Miraculously, though the party was prematurely over, nobody suffered any serious harm, and Leeza and Ravi were able to get up from their tablecloth purdah soon enough. The next day, all the newspapers would report that Hana had gone loco because she was suffering from Former Columnist Post-Stress Disorder. One expert on a newscast added that he thought the gunwoman, once highly coveted, was suffering from Acute Early Success Inflammation.

And though Leeza had seemingly escaped altogether unharmed—she'd even suggested having fries at that new hot spot Tall Poppy Syndrome immediately after—Ravi felt more than a little guilty that he'd let any of this happen. (Gosh, what would Mr. Darcy say?) Mattressing this feeling, however, was the giddiness that Ravi felt about winding up with what might be one of the biggest stories to ever come out in popland. What a scoop! Obviously, though, he needed to get Leeza to tell him more—perhaps in more comforting environs? For all of these purposes and more, he decided it was best to whisk his almost-starlet away on a trip.

"Guess what?" he said to her the next morning.

She jumped to attention.

"We're going to Dubai!"

Her eyes wavered with some middling interest.

"There's a film festival that's starting right about now, and the sheik there is very big on it. Wants as many journalists to come as possible, to help spread the good cheer about the United Arab Emirates. I think we need to get out of town at the moment—I mean, there are crazy literary killers out there!

"Plus," he went on, "we can talk a little more on the flight about that thing you told me. Y'know, underneath the table-cloth? I mean, darling, we'll have twelve hours or so to get into the real meat of it. We can get on the flight tonight."

Dubai beamed liked the cords of a golden harp, shimmered better than Beyoncé's hair. Dirhams cascaded from the sky like confetti. The whole sheikdom, it seemed to them when landing in the Middle East a day or so later, was on uppers—always in climax, constantly in frenzy; its skyline throwing up the mirage of going on forever when, truthfully, it was actually a small and rather contained place.

The mirage that was Leeza Pellegrino also refocused itself during their time together on the plane. While enjoying the fruits of first class on Emirates Airlines, a.k.a. Air Nirvana (the easiest way to fast-track to heaven without going through that whole business of dying), his ally in travel relaxed enough to tell the whole lurid story. Sometime between indulging in the treasure trove of snacks before the first of seven meals (served, of course, on fine bone china), surfing the airline's 1,300-channel entertainment universe ("There's, like, a whole Will Ferrell channel!" Leeza exclaimed), and testing the fully reclinable padded seat (the one that slides into a bed better than you have at home), she slowly but surely baby-stepped her way into the truth.

When she said she was an Olsen Triplet, she'd meant just that.

Olsen. Triplet.

To drive the point as home as it was going to go: Mary-Kate and Ashley were her sisters. There had been three girls initially, but through an incredible confluence of events—a switch at the hospital, a barren friend of the Olsen family, the decision to stick with two rather than three—one had been separated from the others. And Ravi was looking right at her.

The other two—her more public sisters—did not know, she spilled. She had only found out herself a few months back. And before he could ask, yup, they were all fraternal. "They call it a polyzygotic birth," she said, reclining on her seat. "More than one egg."

As she settled into a sleep on that gorgeous reclinable seat, Ravi studied his protagonist's face and saw things he previously had not. There was an acute Olsen-ness about her, now that he scoped it out closely. There was something about the space between her eyes, and the particular alpine slope of her nose. A child-woman quality that not only corresponded to the skin-and-bones nature of her frame—although there was that—tempered by the haloed ghost-like thing that seems to come with being an Olsen.

He turned on his overhead light, adjusted his seat, welcomed a flight attendant bearing a silver tray of perfectly arranged star-fruit. "Please, don't mind if I do." Yes, he thought, picking at the fruit, looking at the apparent triplet dozing there in a forest-green Roots sweatshirt. There was a dogged ambition about her, coupled with a capacity for boho barefoot on sand, topped off with the preening yet precarious soul of a lifelong performer.

Did Ravi believe her? Put it this way: he didn't *not* believe her. What kept him awake, though, even after he'd turned off that overhead light, was the thought of what Mr. Darcy had to do with any of this. Knowing him, he'd probably be at the Dubai airport, holding up a sign for them at the luggage carousel.

Mr. Darcy, as it turned out, wasn't at the terminal where they landed, but there was the biggest, most supersized Christmas tree they had ever seen.

"I totally forgot that it's going to be Christmas in a few weeks," yawned a groggy-sounding Leeza. Indeed, so had he. But Dubai, a place peopled by a population composed of ninety percent Sunni Muslims, apparently had not. "Jihad Bell Rock!" That is what the whole airport seemed to be incongruously shrieking, and by the time they got to their lavish hotel in a metropolis once described as "the capitalist dream on steroids," the picture was all but complete.

Checking in, he and Leeza caught the automated piano tinklings of "Winter Wonderland." Oh, quite. They traded faces.

It got better, stranger, whatever, when the next tune out of the self-playing piano turned out to be the considerably less secular "Joy to the World." Indubitably, there was an even more supersized tree here in this lobby, giving off the look of lumber so posh, it flashed like it had been art-directed by Jean-Paul Gaultier. Sitting at a table right under it were various Arab men in clouds of white robes and traditional headgear talking, in hushed tones, with, it seemed, a Crest White Strip–using African dictator.

"Do you do pedicures?" Leeza was already making friends with the concierge, getting all the information that her heart and her nails desired.

Ravi, meanwhile, took in the expensive, harem-ready digs. The hotel was called the Burj Al Arab, and besides being the oldest symbol of the new Dubai, it was also known far and wide as the "world's first seven-star hotel." In actual fact, there was no such thing as a "seven-star" ranking and, as Ravi had heard, some clever marketing person had abracadabra-ed the whole designation. Effusively, it had stuck.

Seven stars or not, it *was* impressive. Like *Blade Runner* meets *Blades of Glory*! Exhilarating, futuristic, and vulgar (but as far as vulgar goes, a perfection of), the place practically spurted with gold. That is, when it wasn't spurting with indoor fountains that would even make Peter the Great blush. From the outside, the building looked like—depending on whom you asked—a sail, a cockroach, a shark's fin, or a mighty penguin. At night, it lit up—just like a Christmas tree!

One of these blinking Yuletide erections also stood, unsurprisingly, near the film festival headquarters that had been set up just minutes from the hotel. Ravi wandered over to where five Middle East minions waited to serve each registering journalist and got himself accounted for and accredited.

Sit, smile, cheese. He had his picture taken. Yes, please, thank you. He was given a list of film times and handed other briefs.

"First time?" asked one of the helpful serfs, a pumpkin head rising out of a handsome robe.

To Dubai, yes. To a film festival, uh, no. He went on to explain to the pumpkin head that film festivals, taken as a whole, had robbed a good chunk of his life to date, especially now, since film festivals had so many lives to rob. Over the past decade or so, extreme Film Fest Inflation had taken root, leading to so many festivals in so many cities all over the world—more than a thousand in any given year—that Ravi half expected to come home one day and find one under way in his bathroom.

In the same way cities and nation-states had once tried to attract skilled workers, or develop natural resources, or at the very least get a Mickey Dee's at every corner, every place now competed for that perfect combustion of celluloid and celebrity to come to town. While the Big Festival Five, according to most, still was made up of Berlin (edgy!), Sundance (scruffy hipster!), Venice (very pretty! quite serious!), Cannes (the Grande Dame!), and Toronto (hefty! people-friendly! big business!), the festival calendar now also screamed out events in places such as Annecy, France (devoted entirely to international animation), Fajr, Iran (the very barometer of Persian cinema), Seoul, South Korea (horror and sci-fi), Hawaii (East meets West on the beach), and Sofia, Bulgaria (an up-and-comer, by festival standards). Some of these festivals had hatched organically. Others were spurred by an urge to keep up with the John Travoltas. Many others, he suspected, had simply been willed into being by various tourist bureaus in their respective countries.

The sheer scope of it—this international chain-gang of cinema—left Ravi feeling a little pinched, not to mention parched. But, on the other hand, it was an excellent alibi for a certain kind of journo looking to get out of town.

Over the next day, he and Leeza, the two world travellers, set off on a mission to see where the plot really met the set design. That is to say, they made a nice game out of trying to spot as many Christmas symbols as they could, here inside the wonderful vortex of the Wild Wild East. The Mall of the Emirates—one of the great malls of the world—proved to be particularly promising. Christmas trees, Christmas carols, and even Christmas specials were generously on hand. Also, a Christmas-perfect fake ski mountain. With a real eighty-five-metre slope, right in the middle of the mall!

Stopping into the inevitable Starbucks, not far from the inevitable skiing, Ravi and Leeza paused to ask the Arab barista what coffees of the day they had. "We have," the barista began, "the Christmas blend—and the Christmas blend."

"Oh, look, there's Santa!" That was Leeza pointing out the man in red, installed in a part of the shopping centre that just happened to be on same floor as the requisite in-mall mosque.

The entire scene, he did have to admit, was varied to the extreme: Brits straight out of *Coronation Street.* Well-fed Indian Romeos. Water-bottle-toting Thais. Hijab-encased Muslim women carrying the latest handbags and sporting the smokiest, most expertly applied eye makeup possible. Seeing Christmas as just another consumerist opportunity—and this, after all, was a country with an actual so-called Shopping Festival, held every January—it was clear that this was just an opportunity to Deck the Malls. And, in a way, with the whole Birth of Christ thing entirely taken out of the equation, where it often gets just a perfunctory nod in parts of the West anyway, it was the purest Christmas he'd ever seen.

Plus, it was the kind of out-of-context experience that Ravi got a kick out of in the same way that, for the professional gossip, the out-of-context celebrity encounter always ranks highest in the pyramid scheme of celebrity encounters. It reminded him of the time he met Salman Rushdie, the world-famous fatwa artist, at an official MTV bash over in France. "What are you doing here?" he'd asked when he came across him among a horde of Euro-younglings, as someone called Grandmaster Flash lorded over the DJ booth. "My son works for MTV," Rushdie said, unfurling his subcontinental Mona Lisa smile. And so it went: from *Midnight's Children* to Kid Rock in a single, galloping generation leap!

Back in Dubai, the afternoon turned to dusk, which turned to a round of camel-milk eggnogs at the bar on the fifty-first floor of their hotel. Ravi and Leeza sat looking out the window, trying to lap it up.

"It's all so fake, isn't it?" she said, looking down. She was referring to the man-made beaches and the end-of-the-world skyline, but Ravi knew—he was intuitive that way—that she was also referring to the plasticity of her own double life. It was with a straw of self-pity that she stirred her eggnog.

And, oh dear, was this bar actually moving? Or did it just seem that way, structured as it was in a full-on circle and fluffed as it was by the same decorator, presumably, who did the Joker's solarium. Ravi's eyes darted as they couldn't help but do when he was out. He noticed, in a corner, that Joshua Jackson, the guy best known for starring in *Dawson's Creek,* and dating Katie Holmes long before Tom and Suri. Here for the festival, possibly? Spreading over the bar like an oral ooze, courtesy of someone's iPod selection, was the not-exactly-new "(Everything I Do) I Do It for You," rasped by Bryan Adams.

Joshua, Bryan . . . darn, those Canadians were everywhere! He had heard, though, that Adams, in particular, is quite popular with the Arabs, whose love for him is bested perhaps only by the Pakistanis, who don't just love Adams, they heart him.

"Check out *those* triplets," recommended Ravi to Leeza, doing his best to get her to look on the bright side. He pointed. She turned her head. And, together, they watched three osteoporosis-prone Chinese ladies, dripping with even more bijoux than Elizabeth Taylor, totter past them.

Yes, it was just that kind of spot. At the bar, on stools, sat two quasi-stallions (possibly Italian, more likely Spanish), one of whom had his fly open. In the mix, at the variety of other tables, were various blonde vivants, various rich suckers, and one could-go-either-way. This latter individual, seated alone, looked like the secret love child of Dodi Fayed and Phyllis Diller, and he/she was spending a lot of time pulling up his/her argyle socks.

Turning their attention next to a table full of Russian mercenary types, it struck both Ravi and Leeza that this, clearly, was not the sort of place to ask whether money can buy happiness or whether the Dalai Lama does make some pretty valid points. So, instead, Leeza asked Ravi if he liked his job.

"I like it at times like these," Ravi told her. "Because, believe or not, I'm working right this very second."

Addressing Leeza's look of confusion, he explained, "I'm exploring the *Zeitgeist.* That's German for the culture. The Germans have all the best words, you know?"

Leeza gave a nod in understanding, or a nod that at least reached for understanding.

"It must be kind of fun being a gossip columnist . . . I mean, I'm sorry . . . is that what you like to be called? A gossip columnist?"

Ravi took a moment. "Honey, I don't care if you call me a gossip columnist or a social columnist, as long as you call me. That's what I always say. On days where I'm feeling fancy, I'll call myself a social portraitist or a society satirist, or maybe just a plain old people-watcher. It can be confusing in the age of the Internet, in this world of Perez Hiltons and TMZs, but I do consider what I do a tad different. People-watcher probably works best. I like the sound of it. Watching people, in a bunch of different situations. There's an element of gossip to it, in the way there's an element of gossip to everything and everyone.

"Look at those guys by the bar," he continued, pointing to the quasi-stallions perched expertly on stools. "Or those women over there," he said, pointing to a certain gratuitous association of blonde vivants. "What do you think they're talking about? I can guarantee you that at least part of what they're talking about is other people. That's what people do. Talk about what other people do. It doesn't matter how rich or poor they are, how young or old, whether they're in a high school cafeteria or in a hospital lab, in a boardroom in Texas or a bar in Dubai. Who is doing what to whom, and do the spouses know? Is her husband as boring as he looks? Is his wife kind of a bitch? Do you think she's getting fat? Have those friends fallen out—and why? Oh sure, they might delve into the occasional exchange about politics, or the exchange rate, or the latest hockey match, but within five minutes, the discussion will likely turn back to the natural rhythms of social life. What have been the rhythms since people appeared on this earth. People talk about other people. I just happen to do it for a living."

"Yeah," said Leeza, interrupting his stirring monologue. "I bet that even cavemen gossiped about other cavemen. About whose cave was bigger, or whose cave was blocking the other cave's view. Or who was doing what in, like, what cave."

It was times like this that Ravi was reminded that Leeza was no cookie-cutter kind of dunce. He clinked his glass of camel-milk eggnog with her glass of camel-milk eggnog.

"And I bet you that even some of those caves had VIP areas!" he put forth. "All it takes is three people for gossip to exist. Two to gossip about the other. And so on." He paused. "But you know, what I love about my column is that it's no beat and every beat. And it's the only subject. Other journalists might cover business, or sports, or books, or music. I cover it all, through the prism of the people that make up those fields."

Ravi now paused, pregnant. A pause worthy of a triplets pregnancy. "If I were to really tell the truth, Leeza, I would say that why I love writing about famous people is that I'm in love with them. I always wanted to know them as a kid, or wanted to live their lives. But now that I know them . . . have studied them up close . . . I don't know . . . I sometimes wish I could go back to just knowing them in pictures. I even think it's time to get out of this whole life . . ."

He stalled, wondered if he'd said too much.

"What would you do?" asked Leeza.

He leaned in, felt his palms dampen. "I don't know. Write novels. Perhaps in Paris! Colour me clichéd, I guess.

"Just kidding, of course," he added quickly with a Cheshire.

"What's the hardest thing about doing what you do?" Leeza had more than one question up her YSL sleeve.

"Oh, it's definitely that trampoline act of being provocative and funny and interesting and still maintaining access. See, I can't really do my job without having access—people wanting to invite me to their parties, people wanting to be mentioned because it validates them in some way, or gives them publicity—but I also can't do my job without poking holes, telling tales. You have a responsibility to amuse and sometimes titillate the reader while still getting the love from the people you actually write about."

"But how do you do that?"

"Well, you can't always. Sometimes I lose my balance on that trampoline. But then tomorrow is another day, ain't it? In general, you do it by being as clever a writer as you can, by saying things without saying them, by writing with a subtext, by reminding yourself that it's better to write in a way so that you're . . . you're, well, reaching for the absurd rather than the plain-out mean. Sometimes you do it by holding back on writing something until a more appropriate time."

"Like the discovery of a new Olsen?" she asked.

They both smiled. He, perhaps, more conspicuously than she did.

"But, seriously, that sounds very stressful!" Leeza chuckled as she and Ravi watched a woman in a Pucci maternity dress waddle her way into the bar and then prop herself up with no worry at all on a stool right beside the two quasi-stallions. He then turned back to his tablemate and closely inspected her. Did she trust him with the information he had about her now? Did he trust himself?

"It can be stressful," Ravi went on. "There's a lot of negotiating I do in my own head every time I sit down to write. The worst part is when you actually get to know or become friends with someone you write about. Michael Musto—he's the longtime gossip columnist for the *Village Voice*—well, he said that it's terrible sometimes to meet an actual actor. Because you meet them, and somewhere back there is a person who just wanted to be an actor, and somewhere is the creative soul that existed before all the money and the power got to them, and then it becomes harder and harder to trash them."

The two quasi-stallions and the Pucci pregnant woman were already in deep cahoots, with a stream of vice-versa laughter coming from their end. In other parts of the bar, the previously mentioned blonde vivants (and even possibly the three osteoporosis-prone Chinese ladies) were shooting them looks that distinctly read: What does she have that I don't have?

"But how do you keep track of it all?" Leeza played with one of her earrings. "I have a hard enough time keeping track of my Facebook!"

"Well, that's just it," said Ravi. "Because I cover the gamut, it's like my head sometimes feels like a pack of cue cards in one of those old recipe boxes. God, you probably don't remember—before you could Google a recipe, let's just say! Not only do I know about Bette Davis—she was before Google too—but I know that her legendary mansion in L.A. is now owned by Carrie Fisher, a.k.a. Princess Leia. I know that it was Randy Spelling—Aaron and Candy's kid—who allegedly first took away Paris Hilton's virginity. I know that Type A is the name of Reese Witherspoon's production company, and that Plan B was Brad Pitt and Jennifer Aniston's old production company way back when. I know that Carolina Herrera—y'know, the designer?—well, she has four daughters, and they're all named Carolina. Yeah, that's how they do it in her family. I know that Mia Farrow was on the very first cover of *People.* I know that Woody Allen and Mia's Farrow son, Satchel, is a genius and started college at fourteen, except that his name is now Seamus, which is what Mia changed it to after all that icky stuff happened with Woody and that Asian girl.

"I know," he finished, "that Ralph Lauren's real name is Ralph Lifschitz."

"Paris Hilton and Randy Spelling? Yeah, I heard that somewhere," registered Leeza. "So, what else?"

"What else what?"

"What else about your job? I'm interested, I really am."

"Is this an interview?" Ravi suddenly remembered that he liked to be the one in the question-asking seat.

"Consider it research for when I'm going to be a world-famous triplet." She stared hard, and then she turned and looked out the window. "It's going to get out," she said. Her tone was nothing if not all wistful. "It *has* to get out."

Which is when a woman with legs so long they probably ended over in Jordan, decked out in a dress that merely bordered on the frontiers of decency, suddenly appeared and stomped right up to their table. Oh, dear, Ravi thought, in that moment getting a darkened feeling. Was the jig up? A jig, any jig?

Was this woman somehow onto Leeza's bombshell secret? Had she been sent here by his dear, dear wife? Could it be, maybe, that she was an angry envoy of the sheik of the United Arab Emirates, wondering why the heck he hadn't actually dropped into the film festival that he'd been flown in to cover and had, instead, spent most of his hours at the mall or having eggnog? All of this went through Ravi's mind.

But the leggy, determined woman surprised him, and more, when the first words out of her mouth were: "Excuse me, but I have two questions. Are you straight? And are you, by any chance, an architect?"

14

The Night Glowed On

"What's it t'you, honey?" warbled Ravi.

This to the intemperate woman standing before their table who was demanding to know right now if he did blueprints and if he did babes. She was wearing something that suggested Chanel, and she looked, Ravi felt, like someone who very conceivably might have a chandelier in her loo.

"I'm sorry, am I interrupting something?" She suddenly stopped, having apparently only now noticed the presence of Leeza. "So, a May-December thing, I'm thinking. Am I right?"

"Ah, no."

"Okay, I know! Your beard?"

"Not really."

"Well, perhaps your daughter?"

"Hardly!"

"You see any architects?" she went on in an inconclusive continental accent. "Preferably straight. But I'll settle for bi. There has got to be one of them crawling around here somewhere. I'm sorry to be going on like this, but I got it bad."

Leeza was confused but amused. Ravi was amused but not confused.

"I figured if I was going to find a nice architect to roll up with, it'd be in Dubai. I mean, look at this place!" She pointed to the Persian Gulf boomtown smiling up at them from their vertigo-enabling vista. "This place is what Hong Kong used to be before the handover. You go to dinner here, and in the space of time it takes for the waiter to take away your dinner and bring a dessert—bingo!—a building goes up."

Leeza hadn't lost her blank look, while Ravi pursed his lips in comprehension. This woman, he discerned, was one of a new-ish species of lady that he liked to call the architect groupie. Or to put it in another way—in the kind of abbreviated manner so appreciated these days—she was an archi-tramp. A sub-genre of diehards he'd come across in his social travels, they comprised an array of women who held out such architectural ardour that they played on the thing that Ludwig Mies van der Rohe, one of history's great builders, once said about God being in the details. To that, these women added the thesis that God is good to the men (and they were mostly men) who make those details.

Professional athletes, in other words, were nice. Leading men actors did the trick. And, certainly, Masters of the Universe business types had their place. But for a woman of a certain refinement and a distinctly twenty-first-century *savoir faire,* architects really did take the cake. The Age of the Celebrity Architect—

something the world has been hearing about ad nauseam ever since the ribbon was cut at Frank Gehry's prized Guggenheim in Bilbao—had led this lady, and more, to the Age of the Celebrity Architect Crush. To them, names such as Rem Koolhaas, Renzo Piano, and Jean Nouvel were as likely to stir their loins as Clooney, Pitt, or Timberlake.

"May I?" asked the archi-tramp to Ravi and Leeza, after she'd already taken the liberty of inserting herself at their table.

He motioned to the waiter to bring over a beverage for the lady and then turned to her and asked, "So, a bad day on the links?" At which point, promptly, he wondered to himself, Just where in the world had he pulled out a *golf* reference? Scary. Very. That had certainly never happened before.

But the archi-tramp didn't seem to mind. "I just came here from Shanghai. That wasn't so bad. It rivals Dubai in buildings going up, pretty much everywhere you look. Practically drowning in architects! I used to spend a lot of time in Berlin—my ex was one of those German constructors—but it isn't what it used to be! Slowed down a bit these days."

Leeza, apparently intrigued, or doing a good job of pretending to be, wanted to know more. "What is it about architects, can I ask?"

"Well, obviously," she exclaimed, "they can get it up!" She said this like it was the biggest gas ever. "But, seriously, young child, I like them because they are both right- and left-brain thinkers. They can go both ways! They have to use their imagination to be really successful, but they also have to use their hands."

"Ah, yes, they're both plodders and ponderers," added Ravi.

"And cerebral and . . ."

"Rumpled and craggy and introverted and aloof! So hot!" He finished it off for her.

A glint went up in the groupie's eyes. Ravi, meanwhile, feasted on visions of not just Howard Roark, the lone egoist visionary in Ayn Rand's *The Fountainhead,* but also George from Seinfeld, who tried, unsuccessfully, to masquerade as an architect to get chicks. He also remembered the time that Frank Gehry, the real-life great in the field, showed off his own Romeo talents during a stop some years ago at Toronto's super-swank Bymark restaurant. At the dinner, his sources told him, the septuagenarian genius charmed the skirts off all the ladies at the table by drawing up customized doodles for each and every one of them. They all fell in love with him, was the verdict. It was love at first draft.

Leeza asked a few more questions. Ravi made contributions from the peanut gallery. Their new friend raved and rattled and elucidated. The night glowed on.

"Well, that was interesting," said Leeza the next day about that interlude in the bar. Or was it the day after that? Time flew when you were collecting frequent-flyer points.

"Yes," he conceded. In actual fact, he would have found it more interesting if something odd hadn't happened, or something strange or eventful hadn't been said. This was par for the course in the Life of Ravi. Wherever he went, people were drawn to tell him things, even if sometimes they shouldn't. He didn't know why. One day, when he was eight, he got lost in a mall, and after wandering around in a daze, an Auntie Mame type with an underactive thyroid found him, took him, bought him an ice cream cone, and then, while waiting for security to find his parents, sat Ravi down to tell him all about how Husband A was wealthy but not nice, Husband B was decent but not rich, and Husband C, recently expired, had been both comfortable and a mensch but did irritate her a little because he never shared the TV remote and didn't particularly like to cuddle.

Yes, people told him things: the confessor to his ear like a wasp at a picnic. It was a blessing that could be a curse, and one that he had turned into a calling.

Back home it was then, soon enough, where the hive presumably lay in wait.

15

Brunch Angst, Brainstorms, and Mahatma Gandhi

"Where have you been?" The words echoed around Ravi in stereo.

Mr. Darcy beat Rory to the punch with the question, but not by much. Ravi and Leeza had just whisked back into Toronto, the titter-totters of their wheelie suitcases providing the soundtrack to their entrance to the hotel. He'd had a feeling he would probably have one or the other, the wife or the vaudevillian, ready to confront at this point—but both of them now?

"I've been getting to know your friend here." Mr. Darcy smirked, sitting in the lobby of the Hazelton. He was wearing a quiet form of indignation, besides his usual sweater vest, which today he had donned on top of nothing, giving just the hint of masculine décolletage. A winter coat swung from one of his hands. Rory, for that matter, had on a curdled smile as well as a pencil skirt.

Dubai . . . film festival . . . Christmas trees . . . really nice Christmas trees . . . stayed at the Burj Al Arab . . . drinks at the bar . . . the Giller Prize . . . the shooter . . . scary . . . really scary . . . life flashing before eyes . . . woman who's mad, mad, mad for architects . . . Emirates Airlines . . . excellent, excellent airline. Ravi let loose the events of the last few days, not particularly chronologically, while Leeza sat down on her carry-on and nodded infrequently.

"Ah, but I see you didn't mention the biggest plot point of all, now did you?" winked and winced our Mr. Darcy. "One plus one plus one equals three. Isn't that right, Ravi?"

"I told him because I thought I was going to die," said Leeza in a defence that came with some distinguished lash-lifting. Mr. Darcy, it seemed, had a way of finding out things.

"Well, I'd love to stay and chat, and get all *Access Hollywood,* but I can't hear another thing unless I put something in my stomach. Obviously, we all have a lot to talk about, and even more to plan, but isn't it best we do it over some nibbles?" This was Rory, sensible even under duress.

"That's a cool idea," said Leeza.

"Yes, outstanding plan," said Mr. Darcy.

"Brunchy?" he added.

Ravi flipped to his phone, looked at the time and the date, and realized it was both morning, thereabouts, and Sunday. "Sounds good. Where to? There's Saving Grace, on Dundas. They do a mean Florentine. And also get in lots of supernerdy boldface, like Michael Cera."

Rory said something about how she didn't really like the feng shui there, to which Mr. Darcy responded by putting out the idea of dim sum—say, at this place, Lai Wah Heen. Leeza said she didn't particularly care for dim sum and whined that what she really had in mind were French waffles. Ravi then suggested a place not far from the hotel called Harbord Room. Rory quickly kiboshed that plan, murmuring that she'd run into too many people she knew at Harbord Room. Leeza asked why they didn't all just go to One, which was right next door. Ravi said something about it being too fancy, and he wanted something down home, especially having just come in from big-bling Dubai. Mr. Darcy threw his two cents in by asking if there was a good place to brunch in Little Italy. Rory asked him if he meant the Little Italy on St. Clair or the Little Italy on College, because the city did have two. Mr. Darcy said he didn't particularly care. Ravi offered a place called Oddfellows. Leeza said that she liked the name, and Mr. Darcy agreed, but Rory said that there would probably be a horribly long wait there. The Rivoli, downtown, for old time's sake? That was Ravi's next suggestion. Rory made a face. Leeza asked if the Brady Brunch, a restaurant just a few streets over, did brunch. Apparently, it didn't.

This went on for a good hour, the to and fro mirroring what happens in so many instances on so many Sundays. What was it about *Homo sapiens* city folk, otherwise competent and quite functioning, when it came to the knotted decision-making that goes into this most sacred of Sunday secular rituals? It seemed to take people longer to make up their minds about their brunch plans than it took Hillary Clinton to get out of the Democratic primary race and finally concede to Barack Obama back in 2008! People who appeared not to quiver an inch about their life partners, their choice of work, and their burning, all-around destinies seemed to get all angst-ridden about brunch. It was a meal that seemed to come with platters and platters of negotiation, and a side of existential mooning, often by people who had had too much to drink the night before. Nora Ephron, the writer, once summed up the midday-eat-on-Sunday scene in her native Manhattan in the following way: "As far as I can tell, the essential quality of an Upper West Side brunch seems to consist of milling in a large group outside of a restaurant for over an hour."

On this particular Sunday, so tired was this quartet from talking about brunch that they eventually lost their appetite for it. Instead, they headed off for the heated rooftop patio that sat on top of the flophouse-turned-cheap-and-chic Drake Hotel, over on Queen Street. There, Cleopatra-ing themselves on a futon-like section, they proceeded to order a round of Bloody Caesars, which, as any adept Canadian knows, is brunch in a glass anyway. Coincidentally, rocker Geddy Lee and thinker Malcolm Gladwell sat just a few laissez-faire futons away, the former's mullet and the latter's jew-fro joining forces for a hairy Sunday montage.

"So let me get this straight," officiated Rory, taking on the tone of a gruff-talking detective in a dime-store mystery. "You're telling me that this girl, this one right here, is the missing Olsen Triplet, except that the world has no idea that there is a missing triplet.

"Is that what you're telling me?" She emphasized her question by taking the celery stick out of her Bloody Caesar and pointing it at Leeza.

"Because," Ravi said plainly, "the world thinks there are only twins."

The subject in question, Leeza, trotted out a look usually

reserved for someone who'd just selected a killer vowel on *Wheel of Fortune.* Mr. Darcy, calm as an anesthesiologist, picked up.

"This is no joke, Ravi. And you, Rory . . . that is your name, isn't it?"

"That's my name," she said.

"Why is she here, anyway?" asked Mr. Darcy.

"She's the brains behind my operation," tried Ravi.

"I can leave if you prefer, Mr. Darcy," stated Rory.

"No, no," rejoined Mr. Darcy. "I have a feeling, dare I say, that you might be useful, Rory."

"So, you were saying?" Rory went on quite usefully.

"This is serious. Dead serious. A good deal is at stake here."

"And the Olsens, they have no idea?" clarified Rory.

"No idea."

"But they will soon?" This was Ravi, probing.

"Oh, you betcha." This was Leeza, gloating. A flicker that Ravi had not detected before panned across her face.

"But at the most opportune time," threw in Mr. Darcy. "We have more leverage if we hit them with this information when they least expect it."

"And money?" asked Rory. "That, I gather, is the end-game here?"

Mr. Darcy now moved his body, shuffling himself into a kind of fetal position. Then he crinkled his nose, offering his very best just-the-facts-ma'am stare. "In the long run, perhaps. But fame is the means to that money end. The discovery of a new Olsen will be a story that will be hard for the world to resist, especially a story about one that failed to get in on the empire that the other two now play in. The sister who didn't get invited to the party."

"Okay, I get it," said Rory. "Poor Little Triplet! That's the storyline we're talking here, isn't it?"

"Poor Little Triplet. Not bad, Rory," commented Ravi, who, it was true, often plagiarized outright from his wife.

"No problem, Ravi." She smiled.

"Sounds about right," said Mr. Darcy, lowering his voice by several notches. "Of course, there will be publicity spinoffs for both Mary-Kate and Ashley. Particularly when the big reunion happens. Preferably at a huge, public event . . ."

"The *Vanity Fair* Oscar party in L.A.?" suggested Ravi.

"There's also the Costume Institute Ball at the Met in New York! In May! The Oscars of fashion!"

"I got it, I got it! The annual Serpentine Gallery party in London! Very, very glam!"

"What about the Kentucky Derby? Triplets and horsies! Could make for a darn good photo-op!"

"Don't discount Clive Davis's big-deal bash at the Beverly Hills Hotel. It's held every year on the night before the Grammys. Solid guest list!"

"The Davos Summit in Switzerland. Totally out of the box!"

"At the Much Music Video Awards! Anybody who's anybody!"

"Hey, what about Whistler? During the big snowboard festival there!"

"At the annual Victoria's Secret show!

"During Art Basel in Miami!"

"Wimbledon!"

There was no end of suggestions, from all four corners of this rambunctious entourage. Ravi started it, but the others carried right along, poring over the jet-set options that rise up in a given calendar year. Ravi had been to and often covered most of these events. Been there, done that, gotten the tip sheet. At one point, eventually, though, Mr. Darcy thought it best to stop this looping brainstorm in its tracks and announced, "I think we might be getting ahead of ourselves."

"You're probably right," agreed Rory, wheels turning. "How do we know if any of this is true anyway? You have my . . . you have Ravi . . . all caught up in this, and I'm not even sure . . ." She was back to pointing her celery stick again.

Galvanized, Mr. Darcy took something out of his trusted murse. A folder, it looked like. He handed it to Rory, who opened it, found some documents, and started to read.

"It's true! It's true!" rang in Leeza. "I'm so tired of standing at fashion shows. I need my front-row seat now."

"It's all there," Mr. Darcy said more casually, pointing to the folder. "All the documentation."

Rory read on, with Ravi looking over her shoulder and Leeza mainly looking at her feet. "I suppose this looks legit," said Rory after a pause worthy of a Patek Philippe. "And I guess we should believe you."

"Actually, you have no choice. That is what is just so beautiful about our new friendship," continued Mr. Darcy, emotionless. "You do know that I know about your little arrangement, don't you? Now, I have some things to confirm on my end. A few things to hammer out. But over the next while, I do have something in mind for you, Ravi." He took this opportunity to point his own celery stick at the journalist. "We are now entering into a new phase where you and Leeza are concerned."

Ravi caught Rory's eye, who caught Leeza's. They all moved into brace position.

"We are entering into something I'm calling Intense Olsen Orientation. That is to say, you will take some time now to teach our burgeoning triplet here all about the ins and outs of Olsen Living. The better informed she is, the better. Preparation is key."

"Intense Olsen Orientation?" asked Ravi.

"Intense Olsen Orientation," repeated Mr. Darcy. "We need the needle moving in that direction. Start with all the tabloid coverage of them from the last five years; you must study the coffee-table book they released. Dig deep. Of course, we'll pay you a little extra for this exercise."

"And me?" asked Rory, with just the softest lining of sarcasm. "Do you have any projects for me?"

"Only that you're there to support your good friend Ravi," confirmed Mr. Darcy with the softest of winks. "And that you refrain from talking to anyone else about this exchange you've been a party to."

"Speaking of party," piped up Ravi. "I just remembered! I have to be at a pretty good one in a few hours. Any interest in going to it with me? We can make it a foursome!"

The party, happening in a semi-clandestine Royal Canadian Mounted Police camp in a seen-better-days part of town, was off and swelling when Ravi and his gang happened upon it. "I can't believe everyone wore costumes," marvelled Leeza. "I thought we were going to be the only ones."

This being one of those December parties put on every year by a world-conquering design firm—a wham-bam event where Christmas shakes hands with Halloween—the columnist and his entourage had arrived equipped. Ravi was in Gandhi mode ("Mahatma Gandhi was the original Diane von Furstenberg!" he'd declared, grabbing a bedsheet and wrapping himself in it), Rory had thought to don a shower curtain ("I'm Janet Leigh in *Psycho,* if anyone asks," she'd said), and Mr. Darcy, who said he couldn't stay long because he had a flight to catch, was working a hair extension and a gigantic, face-hiding fan, all of which was meant to evoke early Karl Lagerfeld ("Before he lost all that weight," he parsed).

And Leeza? Feeling that there is no time like the present for Advanced Olsen Method Acting, she'd grabbed a garbage bag and made it work for herself. ("Mary-Kate would probably wear this and then get a magazine cover out of it!" she remarked, not entirely lovingly, of one of her sisters.)

"Ravi-oli!" A voice seemed to come out of the ether. "Ravi-oli! Is that you?"

There she was, that blonde piece of work he had run into a few weeks back. He forgot exactly where now. Sunshine vomited out of her copiously lipsticked mouth, and her get-up tonight appeared to involve one of those Herve Leger bandage dresses that younger women had been caught wearing in recent years. It wasn't a costume per se, but with the second-skin affect that this particular dress seemed to be producing, she was doing a good job of summoning up a look that seemed to say: Hey, I'm a hooker without a heart of gold. Her breasts hung like two scoops of fro-yo blobs.

"I just love this sheet that you're wearing!" she continued on her end. "It must be Pratesi! A man of your standing wouldn't be caught wearing any other kind of sheet, now would he?"

"And you," she said, zeroing in on Leeza. "That bag is just tremendous!"

"I'm so GLAD you think so," said Leeza very, very slowly. Hanging out with Ravi had evidently made her pun-contagious.

"Lunch soon?" the woman blared, going right up to the newspaperman's face before clucking off fast on her heels. "It's just been ages!"

"Wouldn't miss it," said Ravi.

Leeza went off with Rory and Mr. Darcy to fetch drinks while he studied the room. There was plenty to study. Some people had arrived at the annual holiday do with what appeared to be mixed salads on their heads; others could be found in Teletubby-ish nude suits, their best bad ballerina gear, and, in one particularly Slavic case, a party-like-it's-2009 Vladmir Putin get-up.

Dou, the infamous hairdresser, was in particularly fine form, sporting a kind of spurious Afro. He'd come to the party as a hotel door, complete with a large Dou Not Disturb dangling from his handsome neck. Also about? That couple who went to everything and wanted to be everywhere. He was slight and glib and in possession of a too-tan scalp that did not stop giving. She was an alarm clock of a person who vacillated between being exceedingly pleased with herself and hungering grotesquely for your two-thumbs-up. They always shook people's hands a little too hard, laughed a little too hard at the end of anecdotes, darted from party to party. Every metropolis, small or large, had a version of this sputtery twosome.

In the mix was that pleasantly same-sex and cheerfully interracial couple giving the party. Crème and Brulegood were the last names they went by, and also happened to be the name of their company. Enjoying their hospitality were various ingénues in heat, at least two stars of TV's *Degrassi,* a dime-a-dozen mansleaze or two, a female nihilist or three, an Olympian who won the gold for sprinting about a decade ago, and the world-taking, weight-shedding, fantastically named Measha Brueggergosman. She was an opera star so good at her own PR she should really have been running Hill & Knowlton. The diva waved at Ravi. Basking in her innate aptitude for high-low—he'd once ended up in a strip club with her—Measha was on the dance floor grooving to the Pussycat Dolls as a flock grew and grew and grew around her.

There were also, he noted, the usual social couples that could be counted on to give and dress up parties: Bruce and Victoria, Michael and Diane, Sean and Shawn, Ben and Cheryl, Joe and Kim.

"I think that guy there is giving you the eye, Gandhi," murmured Rory into Ravi's ear. She'd crept up behind him again and was now pointing to a fella prepped to go to a South Beach rave.

"Ah, perhaps he just has a thing for gentlemen who practise non-violent civil disobedience."

"Can we go now?"

"We just got here."

"A rose is a rose is a party," said Rory.

"You know I have to work."

They both laughed knowingly. Then they moved directly behind a stage of gold-painted go-go boys so they could confer just a little more privately.

"What did you think of our meeting today?" Ravi asked, his eyes wandering over to Leeza and Mr. Darcy, who seemed to have found the dance floor and were busting out some serious moves to "Let's Get This Party Started." Before Ravi could respond, though, he smelt the smoke. Brulegood, one of the party-giving design deities, had evidently caught on fire. To be precise, his press-on wings were smoking. The ones that he had on as part of his archangel routine.

"It's his wings!" yelled a certain drunkzilla, as a pitter-patter of omigods went up. A bunch of good Samaritans blew out the offending candle and then proceeded to yank off the burning objects. This was followed by a native-dance-style stomping by two women who home-schooled their children but today were dressed up as cheerleaders. Two party photogs jostled to get a shot of the wings, licked by flames, while others, blissfully ignorant, continued to boogie to an extended Pink.

"So, about our meeting today," Ravi eventually resumed, turning back to his shower-curtained spouse.

"Well," she said, "I think we're playing with fire to some extent."

"And?"

"And I have suspicions bigger than the September issue of *Vogue.*"

"But?"

"Well, I suppose with the money he's giving you"—she pointed to the hands-in-the-air Mr. Darcy—"plus the fact that you have the opportunity to make triplet history, plus you have this thing about always being in the middle of everything, I guess it's clear that you have to stay with it." She paused, thinking to herself for a second and looking over at Leeza. Her voice was slow, like honey. "You're not . . . I mean, you're not attracted to this Leeza girl, are you?"

Ravi gave her an oh, Rory look. "Not my type," he said.

And there, as his bedsheet brushed up against her shower curtain, he felt the flicker of a spark that occurs irrespective of wayward candles and flammable wings. He could also feel a distinct throb forming beneath his Gandhi sheet.

"You do your rounds," she said. "We'll rendezvous later."

16

Spiritually Landlocked

The weather grew more and more petulant. Christmas came and then it went. Watching the snow sulk outside her window one January day, Leeza swung her legs onto a desk and tried to offer her full attention. Intense Olsen Orientation was in session.

And the star pupil, dressed today in Hepburnesque slacks and turtleneck, complemented by thick, ready-for-study-group-at-the-Sorbonne specs, was trying to keep up.

"Did you watch all ten of those episodes of *Weeds*? The ones in which Mary-Kate guest-starred recently?" Ravi was checking on homework.

"I'm on episode eight," said Leeza begrudgingly. "I think. Maybe it's seven."

"Okay," sighed Ravi. "Any thoughts?"

"I think Mary-Kate is better at being Mary-Kate than she is at acting."

Ravi levelled his gaze and sighed again. "Might be true, but it's what happens when you've been famous, more or less, since you came out of the womb. Your life is your movie, and you become bigger than any part."

Leeza sank deeper into her chair, turning an unbecoming shade of sad. Ravi, for what's it's worth, instantly regretted brining up the word *womb.* That wasn't very nice, now was it?

Together for some time now, he and Leeza had been driving through the long and winding roads of Olsen trivia. She had started off with all the enthusiasm of Bill Maher at Sunday church but seemed to be getting into it as the time passed. And unbelievably, at least to Ravi, he had become the one thing he'd never expected to be: an Olsenologist. Mary-Kate's favourite band? Led Zeppelin! Ashley Olsen's granny hobby of choice? Knitting! Apparently, she's just mad about it. These two factoids, among a frenzy of others, were divined, obviously, by reading copious interviews. Both twins grew up horseback riding in their native California. Both have a thing for sweets. Both have exceptionally well-designed pouts. Only one—Ashley—seemed to regularly comb her hair.

Get this, Ravi had instructed Leeza on another occasion. Before Greek shipping heir Stavros Niarchos was Paris Hilton's fiancé, and later ex-fiancé, he was with Mary-Kate. At one point, she also went out with the son of Dreamworks studio founder Jeffrey Katzenberg, i.e., David Katzenberg, who once also dated Nicky Hilton. And round and round the risibly romantic wheel went, the way it does more often than not in Hollywood.

Ashley, for the record, had a thing with Jared Leto, who once dated Cameron Diaz, among other starlets. Although, it was worth noting, she wasn't above dating civilians, as she'd proved when she dated a quarterback—yes, just a quarterback—at NYU.

Both had glamorous internships when they first moved to New York—Ashley with designer Zac Posen; MK, as she's sometimes known, with celebrity snapper Annie Leibovitz. Both of them, together, as part of the many cogs in their twintastic empire, had once launched a toothpaste of their own, courtesy of the makers of Aquafresh. It came in a pump-dispensing tube, and at the time, one magazine chirped thusly about the product: "Tomorrow, the world. Today, the molars."

At times, it all seemed like a mosaic of numbers where the world of the Olsens was concerned, digits blurring into other digits frolicking like friends with other digits. 40. The total number of video titles that the two girl-gremlins appeared in as kids. 30 million. The number of copies of videos that they actually sold. 29 million. The number of books that they'd colluded on and coerced upon the world. 6. Their tally of music albums, selling at a nice, brisk 1.5 million. $40 million. Their total estimated fortune, as fingered not so long ago at all by *Forbes.*

Theirs was a world of PlayStation games and designer jeans and twincentric bed linens.

"This is a good one," Ravi said one day as Leeza sat eating edamame from a bowl, chewing coquettishly. He was reading out loud an article published a few years ago in England, which crowed, "They are not producers, although they are co-producing *New York Minute,* the youngest people ever to produce a film of its size. They aren't singers, although they have released a load of albums. They are not Internet celebs, but they have the most popular teen destination website in the world."

They weren't publishers, or fashion designers, really. Not even actually actors, despite their famous sitcom. What they were, at least according to the article, was "the sum of all these things." The second biggest "child, tween, and teen brand" that the world had ever seen—after all things Disney. Unbelievably, unlike the au courant Miley Cyrus, they had done it all without the backup of Walt.

"Oh, and another thing," Ravi said on another day as Leeza poured a stash of Ravi's Emergen-C into two twin glasses of water. One for her, one for him. The instructor here made use of an easel he'd set up on which he'd pinned pics of both famous Olsens. "The way a lot of people see it, Ashley Olsen is our girly-girl; Mary-Kate is the bohemian. Ashley is our blonde over-achiever; Mary-Kate is the *Grey Gardens*-come-lately."

"So, what will I be?" asked Leeza with typical triplet angst.

It snowed and snowed and snowed that week.

On a grey afternoon, they went to a skating rink that proudly squats right outside of the City Hall. There, underneath a rinky-dink sky and a sole-dampening drip, they found a bench and sat. This was one of the places that Ravi occasionally liked to go to hide in plain sight, as the rink was so glaringly public no hipsters would ever be caught dead there, let alone the cognoscenti. On this day, that old national anthem "If You Could Read My Mind" by Gordon Lightfoot was belching from the speakers. Just one lone couple was on the ice, doing their capades, as Leeza and Ravi sat quietly watching.

"They're kind of cute," she observed, sitting up in a kind of tea-party posture. "Two's a nice number, isn't it?"

Ravi was struck by Leeza's tone. The chill in it was as lugubrious as the weather. To his mind, she looked, at this moment, particularly wistful, even spiritually landlocked. When they'd started their Olsen-study interlude, had either of them thought they'd be delving into such unexpected depths?

"Mary-Kate and Ashley would probably have on their animals right now," said Ravi, after a suitable silence. He thought it appropriate just now to say something foul about the "enemy" and was referring to the skins that the Twins seemed to relish so very much and that had long made them a target of PETA. Though they were known these days for being uncanny fashion-influencers—Dior's John Galliano had used them as muses for at least one collection—that official fur-fighting group took such umbrage at the Olsens that they once based an entire campaign around them, declaring them "evil" and dubbing them "The Trollsens." A statement from the group went out to the media that read, "No one would argue that Mary-Kate and Ashley could use some meat on their bones, but the last thing they need is hair on their backs."

"Ravi?" asked Leeza, showing her prized ability to miss the point.

"Yes?"

"Do you think I'm fat?"

This gave Ravi an excellent opening to tell Leeza about the Great Barista Scandale that had once befallen the Olsen Twins. Mary-Kate and Ashley had, of course, laughed it off at the time, but the mags had insisted that an employee at the particular Starbucks they frequented had secretly been trying to fatten up the stars—by substituting their usual skimmed milk with a full-fattie version! According to *OK!,* the alleged barista in New York was "concerned" about their respective skinny frames. A rep for the girls had quickly deigned to blast the claims, insisting that the story was "ridiculous."

Proving her own valour, Leeza had a chocolate chip machiatto when she and Ravi went to a Starbucks later that day. And she enjoyed it thoroughly.

Together, they ferreted out some more Olsen truths by spending an afternoon watching *New York Minute,* the one feature film that the Twins had collaborated to make. Shot in Toronto, as Ravi was all too wise to, it gave him a chance, as well, to point out some of the sights to Leeza.

The film, which also features Eugene Levy, hadn't done much to knock *Citizen Kane* off the Best Film charts and may just have succeeded in redeeming both *Swept Away* and *Glitter.* "Sugarless gum has been marketed with more wit" is how a critic at *Entertainment Weekly* sized it all up. A "cinematic human rights violation" is how another observer put it. An alleged screwball comedy, its plot seemed to pivot around the girls doing the adventures-in-Manhattan thing, putting the two'fers through various stages of face-mugging, booty-shaking, and fan-base-crossing-over undress.

"Well, that was awful," said Leeza when it was all over.

"You have to understand," he tried reiterating, "that the Olsen Twins are much more skilled at being celebrities than actors. It's a certain skill set," he added, putting a special emphasis on the *s* in both *skill* and *set.*

Which is when the tutorial seemed, irrevocably, to shift away from the particularities of the Olsens to the wider themes of fame and celebrity. "What is about fame, Ravi?" she asked. Fame could be a curse, he told her. Fame could change you. Fame, he said, is what David Bowie said it was, i.e., it "can take interesting men and thrust mediocrity upon them."

A loose strand of Leeza's beautiful, glossy hair fell on her face. Her forehead was glistening.

"Do you know what Eric Clapton said?" he asked her. "'The toughest thing about being a celebrity is being polite when I don't want to be.' The late, great Paul Newman once said that he doesn't think he's 'Paul Newman,' at least in his head, and that's probably what saved him."

This train of thought kept on choo-ing. "In 1978, a nice Canadian girl from the Northwest Territories, Margot Kidder, was picked to play Lois Lane in the big-screen *Superman,*" he went on to tell her, sounding shamelessly swami-ish. "In 1979, she was on the cover of *People.* In 1981, she was on the cover of *Rolling Stone.* In 1996, she was found in someone's bushes in Los Angeles with her teeth missing. She had been living in a cardboard box and had made a homeless friend named Charlie. Margot went from being on the top of the world, from going to beach parties in Malibu and palling around with Jack Nicholson and being on everyone's A-list, to a measly cardboard box. She says she had depression and was bipolar. A few years ago, I wrote about Margot Kidder hawking photos of herself at something called the Big Apple Comic Book, Toy & Art Show. When she was asked why, all she could say was, 'You sell your autographed pictures and you take the money.' She's gotten help, and hasn't had a mental episode since, she says, but she pinches herself about her career. She said, and I quote, 'I was okay. But I wish I had more training. I didn't have the chops.'"

"Sad," murmured Leeza.

"You know what?" he mustered a little later. "Britney Spears doesn't shock me. The late Anna Nicole Smith—may she rest in bombshell peace—she never shocked me either. Courtney Love, Whitney Houston, what's new? Stars rise, they fall. What shocks me is someone like Natalie Portman."

Leeza waited for him to finish, to tell her more about the milky, magna cum laude-ed Queen of *Star Wars.*

"The fact that she's stayed level-headed and seems relatively normal, that's what shocks me more than starlets who show their panties and dance on tables and begin to look at their own bodies as holograms. It's so easy to be snarky and dismissive about these modern deities"—Ravi stopped when he said the word *deity*—"but it's amazing, actually, that more of them don't lose their minds. Especially given the bubbles they live in, and the extreme shortage of oxygen available in their worlds."

He told her the story he'd heard once about Portman. The one in which she and a journalist were seated in a restaurant in Barcelona. The one in which a Spanish lady suddenly appeared, presenting herself at their table and clamouring to get a celebrity doodle. Though Portman obliged, she did not do so without cringing. At which point, the journalist suggested she become a writer because even Nobel Prize–winning writers don't get recognized. "Yes, but if they did," the actress replied, "that would be okay because it would be for their work, something they'd actually done. That woman probably hasn't even seen my films—she's just read about me in a magazine while she was waiting to get her teeth done."

A pale, muted light leaked from a skylight in the main art gallery in town, where Ravi and his New Best Triplet were found traipsing the following afternoon. They hadn't planned to visit, but they'd been walking on Beverley Street, and it seemed as good as place as any to warm up. "Let's wander inside." That's what Leeza said, her apprenticeship in winter going even better than her apprenticeship in all things Olsen.

Recently reopened after a smashing redo or, in this case, a smashing re-Gehry—as Frank Gehry was the one who led the change—the gallery had the soft, non-threatening lines of Zac Ephron's rhinoplasty. Parts of it sparkled like a caramelized sea scallop; a winding movie-scene-ready staircase loomed up from the centre. A Cézanne nodded at them from the corner of one wing. A Henry Moore sculpture drew them into another. There was a command performance by the Group of Seven in yet another.

"They were really, really famous in their day," Ravi advised Leeza.

"More famous than the girls on *The Hills*?" she asked.

"About as much," he replied, thinking it a suitable answer.

Reapplying her lipstick, Leeza stood for several prolonged minutes staring at a painting by Willem de Kooning. "There's something about this one," she soothed. Ravi had a closer look. It was called *Two Women on a Wharf.* And there was something about it. A bitter, brilliant poignancy.

"Maybe there's only room for two on the wharf." That's what Leeza said next, in a way that seemed like her inner voice had gotten inexplicably out. Now Ravi was no psychiatrist, but he knew what shrinks like to call "transference" when he saw it.

"Oh, Leeza. Do you want to go to Starbucks and talk about it?"

"Actually, it would be nice to just go home."

"The Second Cup, then?"

"No."

"This whole Olsen thing is getting to you, isn't it?" he continued. Gentle, gentle, gentle.

"It's just that . . . oh, Ravi, I don't know who I am! I mean, like really, who am I?"

Ravi nodded thoughtfully. He recognized the symptoms that Leeza seemed to be demonstrating. As much as she was a special case, her angst was not so different from the quarter-life crisis that was all the rage among so many, many twenty-somethings these days.

That night, it was Ravi's turn to have a crisis. A crisis, that is, of sleep. He tossed and turned in bed and couldn't stop having nightmares. He had one dream about a party that the Olsen Twins threw in Saint-Tropez, and everyone, just everyone, including Eric Clapton, Paul Newman, and Cameron Diaz, came. Prince Harry, the ginger-haired second-in-line, was there too, as was Margherita Missoni, of new-generation fashion fame. Leeza wasn't invited, and she was very sad, and she stayed back in Toronto, listening to old Gordon Lightfoot songs. He had another dream of Leeza stuck on a wharf by herself, and of Natalie Portman and Anna Nicole Smith and Margot Kidder passing by her on a beautiful sailboat. Italy's Lapo Elkann, the great Fiat heir—best known for inheriting all of his granddad Gianni's suits—was, for some reason, behind the wheel of the boat. And although Leeza called and called their names, neither Natalie nor Anna Nicole, nor Margot nor Lapo seemed to hear, and so she was doomed to sit on that wharf forever and ever. He had a dream in which Leeza was in torn-up rags and appeared to be scrubbing floors, while Mary-Kate and Ashley sat above her on two twin thrones, wearing outfits from their line, The Row. They smelt like roses and sipped skinny lattes.

(What Ravi didn't know until later is that Leeza had some of these same dreams. Some of them even quite a bit scarier.)

Prying open his eyes in the morning, Ravi walked to his door to pick up the newspaper—because, well, it never did cease to thrill him to see his byline in print—and was surprised, just a little, to see that an envelope with his name written on it was propped up on top of that day's paper. Ripping open the envelope, he found a note, written on nice card stock in Leeza's unmistakable chicken scratch.

"Dear Ravi," it started. "I'm so sorry, but I just don't think I can do this. Thank you for your friendship and for teaching me so much, but after further consideration I'm just not sure if I have it in me to be an A-list celeb. Yours, forever fondly, Leeza Pellegrino-Olsen."

17

"Do You Know What This Party Is For?"

"It's all about your brand. I'm a brand. Are you a brand?"

"Gerry, Heather! How nice to see you. Read any good books lately, Heather?"

"He's pretty doable, but I keep being propositioned by younger and younger men. By year's end, I'm likely to be dating someone in utero."

"I was reading an article about how dyslexics make really great entrepreneurs, and I thought to myself, well, duh, that makes total sense."

"Amoryn, it's been ages! Have you met my husband, Lowell? Lowell and I are having a house-cooling next week. You should drop by! We would love to have you. You know you and your camera are always welcome. The food will be great. I told my caterer: I want basic, basic, basic. Nothing wasabi-crusted. Have you noticed how everything seems to be so wasabi-crusted these days?"

"Belinda, you she-devil, you! Where have you been keeping yourself lately?"

"Psst . . . see her? I call her the black miso cod in the family!"

"I never really thought I'd wear pleats again, but I was just in Paris, and the cool-looking guys are wearing pants with pleats."

"Me, I love snail mail. Don't you love snail mail?"

"You, O'Regan! Loved your interview with Gates! Say, have you been working out?"

"Isn't it amazing what's happened to Lord Ivory? Even though he's been convicted, he insists on writing those yammering columns for the paper. Poor Lady Ivory. She seems to have totally disappeared from the scene. She's gone Osama."

"It's true what Sharon Stone once said: 'You can only really sleep your way to the middle.'"

"I think it's so amazing how you're letting yourself go grey. It's so Jamie Lee Curtis-slash-Emmylou Harris of you."

"It was wonderful bumping into you, but if you'll excuse me, I see a wasabi-crusted shrimp with my name on it."

All around Ravi, there were muffles of sound. Some of it with no rhyme, some with even less reason, and a good chunk of it coming toward him in such a way that he saw words, but not lips, and where he did see lips, he saw no words. The lips and words were keeping separate addresses. Sitting in the creamy-lemon sectional sofa of some Important Person's house, he sat perfectly cushioned by several incomprehensible social critters. The lighting was penumbral, the decor was tasteful; the catering, honestly not bad. And Ravi, if you could believe it, was feeling a rare and indigestible gloom.

"So, Ravi, tell us, what have you been up to?" asked the woman on his left, whose hotness was aided by some emperor's new clothes and who seemed to be wearing Katherine Heigl's latest scent, which, gelled with her particular body chemistry, came off like one of those pine tree air fresheners found hanging from a Dodge Caravan rear-view mirror. Many years ago, before this particular incarnation of his, she had been a Good Friend (or at least one of those Acquaintances who, because of sheer proximity or a basic laziness to resist, had ended up in the Good Friend Box, but whom he'd always known, deep down inside, if he was really being honest with himself, was one of those Good Friends with a cut-off date.) Now, divided by time plus his social distractions, she emphatically fit into the Acquaintance Box. And her question, when it came, reached out gloved in contempt.

"Oh, not much," he said with the easy liar's smile.

"Oh, really?" she replied with a return smile that made clear that she appreciated the lie. Some people, especially those like her, didn't really want to hear about his non-stop carousing, his nocturnal adventures, and his medley of run-ins with celebs. He'd learned this lesson early on, and he only felt it right to respect it.

It was the kind of acquiescence that was a crucial social skill: pandering by omission.

His attention drifted back toward the growing throng, and he let out an inward sigh. Where would he start, anyway? He went to more parties in a week than most people go to in a year, and, all things considered, he could easily stop cold turkey right now and still beat most people's life counts. Was it nice to tell her that, just last night, he'd had dinner with that famous crime novelist and also attended a party in honour of that not-unfamous singer? It was one thing to tell people in his column, behind the veil of the byline, but it was another to come clean face to face. Would he then also go on to tell his demoted friend that he had had—oh so briefly—custody of a not-ready-for-prime-time Olsen triplet, whom he'd been given strict responsibility for, but whom Ravi had proceeded to, well, accidentally misplace?

"What do you mean you've lost her?" That had been Mr. Darcy's predictably pinched response when he'd called him to tell him the not-so-great news.

"Well, she's around, I'm sure," he'd squirmed, going on to tell him about Leeza's goodbye note.

"Ravi, this is not good," he'd said, his phone voice making like the antithesis of sparkling.

"You have to find her." This was Mr. Darcy's directive, after more of the more or less had been divulged.

Listening to the columnist splash around in a vat of shame, the Jane Austen–inspired know-it-all had gone on as follows: "Ravi, if you don't find her, you will leave it to me to spill the details of your marital union. And you know what happens then."

Ravi's instinct was to keep it cool, to play the I-know-that-you-know circle jerk. "I wouldn't begrudge you for it, Mr. Darcy. But I don't think it's going to get to that point. Give me a few days, I'll find her."

A few days, however, had turned into a few weeks, and though Mr. Darcy and he had kept in regular check—threats, both subtle and italicized, were made—the situation had reached stalemate status. Leeza's phone had been disconnected. Her Facebook gone untouched. And not only were the clock ticking, the die cast, and the jig quite evidently up, Ravi, who liked to leave no cliché unturned, had come across a tabloid pic of Ashley and Mary-Kate going into the Beatrice Inn, in New York. Naturally, this brought up a rush of memories and compelled him to start practising his camera-ready grief face. It was important to be prepared, after all, if it all blew up, and the women from *The View* came calling. He could also see the *US Weekly* cover now: The Triplet That Got Away!

Indeed, so hard was this third-act woe with Leeza—they'd met, they'd bonded, she'd bolted—that Ravi was unable to write his column for three, going on four, days straight.

"Just recycle some old ones," he'd told Sam, his editor, when he'd called to explain that he was "ill."

"Oh, Ravi, not again," the newspaper-minder had grumbled. "You know how I hate it when we have to do that."

"Sam, it's not like we do it *that* often. Just change some of the names. One boldface is another. The scenes change, but the names they go on. And half the time all people are doing is perusing for the names anyways. The verbs and stuff, they're beside the point. Trust *moi:* nobody will know the difference."

Nobody did.

"She got cold feet," his dear Rory had said when she'd tried comforting him about Leeza. "This was like a big wedding, and she just wasn't ready to commit to being an Olsen. She's like a runaway bride, but she'll turn around. I bet you she's flagging down a FedEx truck as we speak, trying to get back to the church."

Ravi always appreciated when Rory used an old Julia Roberts movie reference to make her point, but even this did not cheer him much. "You don't think"—he'd turned around and looked

Rory in the eyes to ask—"I mean, you don't think she would have done anything. Done anything horrible, do you?"

"Don't be ridiculous!" Rory said, taking his hand. "You know that Leeza is just having an acute case of that thing you've long noticed about celebrities!"

He waited for her to finish the thought.

"Wake up and smell the chai, Ravi! It's called Imposter Syndrome, and you're the one always telling me it's an epidemic. Not only in Hollywood, but anywhere you find the rich, the fabulous, and the near-fabulous. That hairdresser's daughter who becomes an overnight starlet. That guy who grew up hand to mouth but is now the toast of the London art world. That kid from nowhereville who has it made now, and just when he or she can afford to buy whatever they want is suddenly—and ironically—being sent free clothes by the trunkload from designers who want the exposure and being offered free stays at hotels that want the association. Imposter Syndrome! Most talented people who weren't born with silver spoons have at least an ounce of it. You're the one who says that it's what gives some actors a certain depth on the big screen! Leeza's situation is pretty peculiar, but it's clear that's why she ran away. She's not scared to be a sudden celebrity. Rather, she's probably scared that she'll be really good at it."

"Did anyone ever tell you that you talk a lot?" he asked Rory, which got the intended rise out of her.

"Don't lose hope. And don't blink where that Mr. Darcy is concerned," she said as part of her last-but-least valedictory address. "By the way," she added, right before torpedoing out of town on another one of her business trips, "did you think to check all the mani-pedi spots, coast to coast?"

Looking around now, sitting at this party, he smiled belatedly at the suggestion. In this basmati-rice-coloured penthouse the size of a new car dealership, he could see the frantic flights of meet-and-greet, all the thwarted twosomes, and the all-too-familiar spectre of those just a rail or three away from twelve-step.

"Champagne?" asked a man with a not-fooling-anyone plough of hair, pouring him some Perrier-Jouët before he'd had a chance to answer. Ravi tried not to grimace and stood up to thank the man, almost hitting that rice-paper lantern hanging above the creamy-lemon sectional that had been his wallow.

"We are so glad you could make it," continued the man.

"Oh, it's my pleasure," said Ravi, wondering what the *we* in "we" actually meant. Was this the man who lived in this basmati-rice-coloured penthouse? Was he the chair or co-chair of this apparent fundraiser that was afoot? Possibly its moneybags? And now that he mentioned it, what was the fundraiser for? Was it even a fundraiser? Ravi had no idea. And if he had once had one, he had promptly lost it. It was classic party amnesia, and Ravi often developed it when he was stressed.

"It's just such an important night," said the man, breaking up his thought chasm.

"Oh, absolutely," he replied.

"And media attention, naturally, never hurts."

"Of course."

"We wanted to keep it fairly intimate."

"It's terrific!"

"You've been familiar with us long?"

"Not as long as I would have hoped," said Ravi, hoping that his vagueness would carry him through the exchange. He was going to say something about "it" being a critical "issue," but then he wasn't even sure if this was an issue. And if it were, would Ravi be for it or against it? Was this pro-animal rights or anti-land mines, pro-computers for kids in Africa or anti-spread of malaria?

"Linda Evangelista has been such a huge supporter. Unfortunately, she couldn't make it tonight," the man went on. Ravi oh-oh-ed appropriately. He also took in again the man's no-fuss mop, which was accessorized, he saw, with a manner both languid and vaguely menacing.

"Linda is quite something," said Ravi, good-naturedly enough, about the Canadian drop-dead who was widely said to have kick-started the 1980s supermodel era but whom he'd actually found vaguely disappointing when he'd sat beside her at a dinner once. Her skin was moon-glowishly lovely, but her mall-girl voice monosyllabic. And her ideal forum, consequently? Definitely the still photo.

But wait? What did Linda Evangelista have to do with this party? Ravi actively skimmed his mental celebrity database. He knew that Linda was very active in raising dough for breast cancer research, so maybe that was it. Or—duh!—could this be a fashion party? Some sort of product launch? Linda had not long ago starred in a Prada campaign. Could that be it?

"More champagne?" asked the man, once again not waiting for a yea or nay, as Ravi eyed the room, looking for possible cues. In the corner, there were two fussy-vampire types in the Armani Exchange male model vein who seemed not to have gotten the memo that Anne Rice was a born-again now and that emo-vampires, in the Stephanie Meyers vein, were more in vogue. Neither appeared to be the marrying kind. Both seemed to be involved in a kind of exaggerated bed-head-off. Not exactly the breast cancer fundraiser demo, but who knew? Ravi had been around long enough to know this might precisely be the kind of party that these types might hit to find vulnerable cougar-prey.

Speaking of the arts, over in another corner were several of those sixty-something gay lumberjack types. One of them was even working—could it be?—his lumberjack shirt with man-pris! Ravi considered the possibility that this event might have a gay angle. The launch for a new collagen? A celebration of a hot new hoofer in a hot new musical? Although possibly he was being a little myopic, as in this age of the post-metrosexual, even a straight was known to wear the occasional micro-pant, wasn't he? Good God, Ravi said to himself, you can be sooo judgmental!

Okay then, how about that status-surfing couple over there. Oh, yeah, it was that same sputtery twosome he saw at almost every party. But because they went to everything and wanted to be everywhere, their presence failed to tell him much. Wrong number, he told himself. Alternatively, there was that self-made non-damsel with the Sarah Palin specs, shadow-husband in tow. What about them? Word around town had it that she had taken whatever gonads he had apparently once possessed and put them in her Coach bag on the day they got married. Knowing the tics of this particular couple, he tried to work it out: what kind of event would attract this particular quality of castrating careerist and scaredy spouse? It was a weekday, after all, and she would be getting up at five the next morning to go for her morning triathlon, dream up a deliciously organic breakfast for her two kids, and, of course, torpedo through the five daily newspapers and eight essential blogs she checked first thing. The point being, it would take a certain calibre of party to get her out in the first place.

His fashion radar went off, though, when he noticed that there was a good proxy here of those TV, radio, and print types who form an unofficial club in this town and who are constantly the sort of media centipedes you'd see at anything remotely material goods related. These were the same types who faced the constant challenge of trying to find new and interesting things to say to one another, because more than likely they'd seen each other the night before. But yet, their yes-logo presence was muddied here by the spectre of the New Left propeller and authoress Naomi Klein. And . . . wait, wasn't that the Marvel Comic–haired Jay Manuel of Top Models, American and Canadian, in deep eye-to-eye with Naomi? Whatever could those two have to say to one another? Either he was styling her or she was schooling him, but whatever it was, out of Jay's mouth now wafted the word *fierce.*

As he tried to wrestle with the possibilities—all the while trying to put sunblock on the Eternal Sunshine of the Party Mind—his eyes rested upon a certain man about town dressed in a *Mad Men* suit. He recognized him. From watching him over the years, he'd definitely deduced that he was one of those competitive-eater types. A foodie of the highest degree. The kind who tended to show off by ordering "off menu" in restaurants and was always telling you at length about his latest biannual visit to Fat Duck in London, or that time, years before *Gourmet* or anyone else was in on it, he "discovered" elBulli in Spain. If he was here, it had to mean something. Was this an olive oil launch? An all-hail to a foreign chef? But, if this was true, he now considered: what were Gerry and Heather doing here? In the alphabet soup of invites, this plush couple was an *A*, and they wouldn't step out for just anything.

Ravi gave an abbreviated smile to his much-obliging champagne-pourer, then screamed inside. There were clues aplenty about what this party was all about. Problem was that all the clues appeared to be contradicting one another. Even the wasabi-crusted shrimps being passed around told a story, and then another. Knowing his caterers better than he knew some of his relatives, he knew these were the work of Dickson & Co., and they typically did events for an avant-garde crowd. This gathering, though, was neither especially *avant* nor particularly *garde.* Not as far as he could see.

He felt—as he so often did at a soiree—like suddenly bursting into song. Just to stir things up. Something Sting perhaps. That one about Roxanne, for instance.

"Olga had to leave. But she wanted me to say hello." This is what the exasperating man uttered next.

"Oh, did she?" said Ravi, wondering who Olga was. "That's so nice."

From the corner of his eyes, he could see that the man in the man-pris was now talking to the man in the *Mad Men* suit. And unless his eyes were deceiving him, the man-pris man was giving Ravi the kind of look that Woody Allen probably gives Scarlett Johansson.

"Well, this has been just great," Ravi said next, thinking this his cue as he began to beeline. "Thank you so much, but I do think I need to punch out."

"*Don't forget to take a gift bag on your way out.*" That's what he heard the man with the champagne bottle screaming all the way down to coat check. "Gift bag! Take! Gift bag! Don't you dare forget!"

Of course, of course, the gift bag.

As Ravi waited for the arrival of his peacoat—what was a gentleman's winter, after all, without a peacoat?—the idea grew on him that the gift bag would provide some insight into the mysteries of this party. How could it not? But when his beloved peacoat and the goodbye sack finally did appear, courtesy of one of those self-loathing coat-check types you'll find in any era in any town, all the bag managed to do was enhance the enigma of the evening.

"It's a watering can. For gardening," matter-of-facted the sassy self-loather who was holding down the coats fort. Ravi tore open the bag, and, yes, it was true. Ostentatiously—because the moment called for it—he held up a beautiful, new, purple watering utensil. Attached was a tag that read, and only read, Thank You for Helping Us Grow!

"Oh, for Pete's sake," said Ravi to himself, still nonplussed but doing his best to be PG.

As he was finally leaving, he ran into the Donatella Versace–haired woman who made up one-half of the local husband-wife paparazzi team that could always be counted on to keep these parties well documented.

"Hey," he said, "can I ask you something?"

"Sure," she said with a nod.

"Do you know what this party is for?"

Nodding again, but this time with an accelerated gum-chew, she said, "You know what, Ravi? I've been trying to figure that out myself.

"But," she added, pointing to a smartly dressed woman in the corner who sat at a makeshift table near the coat check, "why don't you ask her? She's the party psychic."

The woman heard this and twitched in his direction. "You're a psychic?" asked Ravi, noticing that she had on a lace of neck diamonds the size of ice cubes.

"You bet your bottom dollar I am. We don't all wear babushkas, you know."

"I'm sorry, I didn't mean to imply . . ."

"That's okay. I'm still getting used to this gig. We moved here from New York when the recession hit in 2008, and my husband lost his shirt. We thought we'd hide out in Canada until it all blew over and the SEC got bored, but it ain't so cheap here—even with your dollar. So I've been offering my gift to those who'll take it. In-party psychics are very big in Macau, did you know? I thought I would give it a try and create a market here. My husband and I, we love your column, Ravi. Never miss it."

"Thank you. Very much. But it is true—we could use some more value-added stuff at parties. They tried sushi-on-naked bodies for a while, but that got old fast. Lots of parties—especially in L.A.—have those classic photo booths so people can duck in and get their pics together, and that's been a hit with some people. But, psychics. What a clever thought. Definitely."

The woman smiled, jangled her jewellery. Then she laid out her cards. "So I see that you're in a hurry. Is there something I can tell you real quick? You have one question, and one question only."

He started to ask her about the ins and outs of this mystery party that they both found themselves at, but then he had an even better idea. One that would make much better use of this Stepford's talents. "Leeza Pellegrino!" he exclaimed. "A friend of mine. She's missing, sort of. I need to find her. Can you tell me where she is . . . Ms. . . . Ms.?"

"Ms. Goldfarb," she answered.

"Ms. Goldfarb."

Her smile came and then vanished. She took a breath. Ravi stiffened and made room so that two women who looked like Nova Scotian lesbians could get by him to collect their bombers. "I'm seeing the number three," announced the psychic eventually, and very quietly.

So far, so good. "Yes, Ms. Goldfarb. That sounds right. But where is she? That's what I need to know."

Ms. Goldfarb started to make what sounded like a gargling sound. And then a follow-up noise that was akin, more or less, to the sound that Mickey Rourke probably emits when he goes rock climbing. "I have it!" she erupted.

Ravi waited for her through an interminable pause.

"I see a website. A website."

"What do you mean?"

"I see it very clear. It's a website."

While the link www.whathasthiswomanbeensmoking?.com flashed before Ravi's eyes, she studied him like he was a bar exam, her mind evidently careening. "WireImage. I see the website wireimage.com."

"WireImage?"

"It is the key to your friend, Leeza Pellegrino. The key, Ravi."

Ravi hesitated, but not much. Taking Ms. Goldfarb at her word, his own mind metabolized her prediction. WireImage, as any partygoer and thrower worth his or her salt is aware, happens to be the biggest online inventory of all the biggest soirees happening day to day. Besides being an in-the-know photo album, it held the distinction of serving up instant social history. Could it be, somewhere, on the site, there was a clue to his Leeza's whereabouts?

"Thank you, Ms. Goldfarb," he said, digging into his pocket to give the woman some Queen Elizabeths.

"I will not take your money," she said, putting out both palms. "Don't you dare pay me." She stopped and then said, "But if you want to boldface me in your column, I certainly wouldn't be displeased with that."

"Done, Ms. Goldfarb," announced Ravi. "You're officially the country's It Psychic. Now, if you don't mind terribly, I have a computer I have to be at."

And with that, Ravi buttoned up his peacoat, waved *arrivederci* with his watering can, and headed out to his next cockamamie chapter.

18

Blowhards, Coat Hangers, and Camera Whores

He spent most of his night, and a good part of the next morning, mousing his way across parties, both present and past. It wasn't a task for the faint of heart, and it had been, so far anyway, far more foreplay than climax.

"Who knew you were such a mystic?" asked Rory when he'd phoned to tell her about the psychic's counsel.

"If you believe in chiropractors, I can believe in psychics," he struck back. "Don't forget, Rory, I come from a long line of Indians, and we practically invented fortune tellers!"

Plus, he had to remind her now, he was a big believer in faces—you had to be when you dealt with PR people for a living—and Ms. Goldfarb's had specifically spoken to him. Even beneath all that Restylane, there had been rectitude. And so he sat in front of the computer, lightly flicking over pictures on wireimage.com, looking for something, although he knew not what.

It was a place he'd been many times before, poring over images on the site the way they examine bodies on *CSI*. Portraits of people so famous that they don't need a caption to tell you their names—Nicole, Leo, Mandela—sat here alongside photographs of less prosaic faces. It was one-stop stalking. Ravi often did this very computer thing after getting in from a hurly-burly din-din or launch, or any party, really. As did anybody who's anybody, and even some nobodies. WireImage—essentially a trumped-up press agency—had in recent years turned into an online Piazza San Marco for those who like to row in and around the canals of celebrity. Sending out armies of photographers to everything that happens in the shindig capitals on any given days—a fragrance launch in London, a cable television premiere in L.A., a diva's birthday in divalicious Paris—the website allowed you to do a variety of things, including these three:

a) look up the people you missed at the party you were at last night because you left way too early or arrived way too late,
b) look up the people you saw but you don't remember now because you had too much to drink,
c) look up the people at the party you told everybody else you were at, but you weren't really, thus giving you the wherewithal to lie with vigour.

Besides all this, it had been said, celebs themselves followed their postings on WireImage the way modern political parties follow the polls.

"Leeza, where are you?" soliloquied Ravi as his eyes set on a holier-than-thou assemblage of personalities, then shifted to a

B-crowd of promiscuous would-bes and went on to an event that was A-list-approved but like so many of these things could look kind of glum and listless in pics. (A picture, after all, was worth a thousand worry lines.) The whole gang was here: chronologically in place, frozen in time. Couples that you never expected to last (Melanie and Antonio) sat next to couples who you'd never expected to attach (Calista and Harrison). There were, for instance, both Tilda Swinton and Tila Tequila, but not together. (The first did very good couture pantsuit; the other, the reality star, was tsk-tsked to be a faux-mosexual.) There, he saw Russell Crowe and Keri Russell, Meg Ryan and Ryan O'Neal, Oscar de la Renta and Oscar de la Hoya! Hey, wasn't that Dr. Dre and Dr. Drew, eking out space with both Tommy Lee Jones and just plain Tommy Lee?

Click. The never-say-die Hugh Hefner standing strong with his latest and greatest harem. Click. The many shirt buttons-unbuttoned Bernard Henri-Lévy, a French intellectual who'd helped to put the sexy back into smart and who had mastered the look of someone always on the cusp of a clever rebuttal. Click. The ubiquitous Eva Longoria, who'd managed to scrape herself out of soapland—hadn't it just been a few years ago when she was playing Isabella on *The Young and Restless*?—and not only fashion herself into the most photographed of the *Desperate Housewives,* but also poof magically into a L'Oréal-contracted, NBA-star-wed BFF of Victoria "Posh" Beckham.

Evangeline Lilly. Adam Levine. Larry Birkhead. Jessica Stam. Fame was always in a hurry here; fame's work was never done. Tony Fireball, Tina Fey, Thandie Newton. Jackie Chan and

Jemima Khan and Eminem. Click, click, click. Some were willing; others looked like they were red-carpet Manchurian Candidates. It made him mull what Simon Cowell had once said about the dirty business that seemed to involve having one's picture snapped. "Anyone who complains about invasion of privacy shouldn't work in the entertainment business," the *American Idol* judge growled in an interview. "You can't have it both ways. It's as simple as that. I think there are too many people at the moment bleating about having a picture taken. Trust me. When the picture taking stops, they're going to be more unhappy. That's the way it is."

Searching for potential Leeza Pellegrino breadcrumbs, Ravi stumbled upon a pic of Imelda Marcos, still going strong, it would appear, on the soiree front. He was too young to exactly remember the reign of the shoe-loving former first lady of the Philippines, but he'd always been fascinated by the old goat. He especially loved the story, way back from the dark ages of 1990, of when Imelda was on trial in New York for racketeering and she would show up in court accessorized with a blood-pressure monitor. The machine had the impeccable timing of gurgling quite violently in the courtroom every time her blood pressure did swell, which corresponded quite nicely with critical points, it was said, in the trial.

And look, wasn't that Uma Thurman with her latest love, Arpad "Arki" Busson? She was the statuesque star of movies like *Pulp Fiction* who'd gone on to yellow tracksuit fame in those two *Kill Bills,* and who'd been married to actors Gary Oldman and Ethan Hawke, and nearly so to famed hotelier

Andrew Balazs, and whose father, Robert Thurman, famously, was the first ever Westerner to be ordained a Tibetan Buddhist monk. He, a British hedge-fund billionaire, was the former consort and baby daddy to Elle Macpherson, and one-time gentleman caller to Farrah Fawcett, and a networker of elephantine acclaim. Ravi looked closely at Uma and Arki's pic together at a thing at Scot's in London to see whether there were any cracks behind their expert smiles. There weren't. As far as couplings go, this one had captured Ravi's attention—partly for the two or three degrees of it all but partly, simply, because it was a big money/big Hollywood merger of the old-fashioned assemblage. It was like when Ted Turner married Jane Fonda, or when Joe Kennedy (JFK's pop) dallied, way back when, with the one, the only Gloria Swanson. But he digressed.

Slipping past any number of lusty blowhards and camera whores and Little Miss Sunshines and porcelain-skinned coat hangers—not to mention Jack Nicholson, out at a golf thing, those parenthetical arches crossing his forehead as per usual—Ravi squinted his eyes at some socialite bobbleheads. That queen of the New York bee, Tinsley Mortimer, was in the picture he was looking at, and it struck him, as it had many times before, that socialites weren't what socialites used to be. Take *Town & Country* magazine, which used to have a policy of using only real woman (read: socialites) in its fashion stories and on its covers, but today, like most of the offerings on the newsstand, mostly used cookie-cutter celebs for their fronts.

Where was Leeza? Was she peeking out from behind one of these marked-down socialites? Sandwiched between trustafarians? Hovering beside those Urban-Kidmans or next to those DeGeneres-de Rossis? Or was that her arm there, innocuously caught in a picture behind that man-banged heartthrob Chace Crawford at party in Vegas? Savouring the possibility, he remembered the time he'd met the *Gossip Girl* actor at a party in Toronto, where his Peter Pan 'do had glistened like the silver spoons you imagine glistening in Ivanka Trump's Rem Koolhaus–designed spoon rack. "Have you noticed that you've set off this whole bangs thing among guys?' Ravi had asked him, trying to light a quote. "No," the It Boy shrugged, not giving him anything he could use. At which point, a minute or two later, Chace came through—like so many of these game-playing celebs often do—and said to the reporter, pointing to the bottle he had in his hand, "I like this beer. I love Canada." Ravi—knowing that banal can sometimes be gold—felt his work for the evening was done.

But, no, Leeza was not here with Chace, and neither, on closer inspection, was her arm.

"Okey-dokey," Ravi said out loud, taking this opportunity to finally take off the Hermès tie he'd been wearing, paired with a dress shirt worn over *Risky Business* briefs. He also took this chance to wander over to his stereo and put on The Clash.

"You're out there," he said, feeling his bluster build as the music swelled. Confidence sometimes just needed a soundtrack. He swung himself back into his chair, bit into a freshly ripped-open Coffee Crisp, and looked deep into the cesspool of celebrity. Why would Leeza be somewhere here, anyway? Easy. It was the same thing they said about serial killers, Ravi figured. As much as it was in their best interest to drop out of sight, they couldn't help but hang around the scenes of the crimes. In the case of his missing friend, she had come so close to stardom, gosh-golly, holy-moly stardom, that there is no way she could have quit it all cold turkey.

It was a theory, anyway.

He kept looking, thinking. There went a jazz-handed, wheelchair-bound Elizabeth Taylor and a honky-tonk, clothing-optional Matthew McConaughey. There was an entourage-less Jeremy Piven (he had become the face of "mercury poisoning," ever since dropping out of a Broadway play due to too much sushi). There was that *Vogue* boss, Anna Wintour, who looked every bit (and more) like Anna Wintour in her never-change precision bangs and a pair of dark glasses that both hid and made manifest her special ilk of Chekhovian sadness.

And that is when his phone made itself known. It was a text from Rory.

"Dear Husband-Person," it began. "Going into a meeting now, but it just occurred to me: perhaps you've got it all wrong!!! Maybe when the psychic said wireimage.com was the key, she meant that Leeza is going to show up on the site soon, not that she already has!"

Next text: "Your best bet might actually be to figure out what events WireImage is sending out cameras to over the next few days. Honey-bunny, I may not be psychic, but I think I'm onto something!!!"

Taking another crunch from his chocolate bar, Ravi had two thoughts. First, he couldn't believe that Rory had used so many exclamation marks in her message to him, especially when she was always telling him he was an exclamation-mark whore in his columns. Second, he had to admit it: his wife truly was a genius.

Actually, Ravi had three thoughts. The third was this: it's time to call George Pimentel. By this, he meant the guy whose dad had been a wedding photographer but who himself was Canada's best-known contributor to WireImage. No stranger to events, from everything like the Oscars down, he was the good-guy paparazzo that everybody back home wanted to be around for their parties. He would have the info. He would be able to tell him what parties around the world were on the website's radar. Of course, just to be nice (and because all is fair in love and wire image), he'd offer up a tidbit to George in return. This was the etiquette, after all, in party-intelligence sharing.

The line rang only once before he heard the gung-ho hunter-gatherer voice of the shutterbug.

"Hey, George! It's Ravi. How's it going? Don't know if you know already, but I'm hearing that Gene Simmons is going to be in town with Canadian wifey, Shannon Tweed, and they're planning on a doing a little light shopping in Yorkville. Yeah, yeah, kind of crazy, but they're one couple that's lasted! . . . Well, I'm sure if you talk to their publicists, they'll let you do a little shooting . . . What'd you say, George? . . . Oh, no problem at all . . . Thanks, that's great . . . Well, my sources say that they're probably going to hit town around 1 p.m. Say, George, if you don't mind, I've got a question for you now."

19

The Scene of the Chintz

The next day dawned gauzy. Which is when Lady Ivory summoned.

"Ravi, if you wouldn't mind, I'd like to see you," she'd said, her voice sounding as ever elegant but also like what the fuzzy side of a lollipop would sound like if it could talk.

Before he could ask where, she adjoined, "At my house. It's important."

Ravi had just narrowed down where he might likely find Leeza—and now this? No psychic needed to tell him that, as far as coincidences went, this wasn't one. So off he travelled into the glasshouse hinterlands of the city, crossing the steel bridge that hovers over the Don Valley Parkway and has its much-storied non-Zen side. Up and up and up. Back to the scene of the chintz.

Hello, Lady Ivory nodded when he got there. Her movements were wary and tight; the mouth, a cul-de-sac. No opera company was going to be casting her as Carmen any time soon.

“You called?” he chimed.

“Sit down,” she instructed Ravi, motioning with both hands to a chinoiserie-covered chaise. Those hands reached out like a sweet pair of silver tongs and now he also noticed that the Lady herself was hunched over a motorized tub, her bare tootsies immersed in its excitable waters. A neither-too-old-nor-too-young woman hovered nearby, mute.

“Thank you,” he said.

The silence protracted. A solitary candle set off shadows. Without the party murmur, and with this beleaguered lighting, the house where he’d first encountered Mr. Darcy, all those months ago, seemed very different. Besides Lady Ivory’s usual scent, there was also a certain Eau de Forlorn at work. Her peepers, in addition, had a vaguely wet quality.

“Reflexology just rocks, doesn’t it?” This is what came pouring out of Ravi as he tried in vain to fill the space.

“The trial has not been good for my feet,” replied Lady Ivory, referring to the legal hullabaloo that had enveloped her white-collared husband. It was ongoing, and provided daily theatrics still. The couple’s fortune was being frittered, it could be said, as they sat.

“Yes, the trial,” he said.

“The trial,” she repeated.

“How’s it going, may I ask?”

“Ravi, we’re looking at all possibilities. I’m not sure what I’m going to do if he goes to jail, but it’s obvious it’s a possibility I have to start entertaining.”

“I’m sorry to hear that.” Ravi offered a mollifying smile.

"Lord Ivory is rich in the scheme of things, it's true," she said, looking around the place. "But don't you think we'd be richer if we were as lawless as they say we are?"

Is she being unusually candid? Sincere? Scheming?

More minutes, more seconds, more thought bubbles. He noticed a pride of black lion figurines on the mantel, ones he hadn't before. Black lacquer, possibly?

"You're probably wondering why I called you," she spoke after a memorable interlude. Her words had a heaviness to them, as if every syllable were being held down by sandbags. And if she had a brow that furrowed, she would have done so.

"The thought had crossed—"

"It's about," she cut in, "our mutual friend. This Leeza creature." Lady Ivory gave a nod to the hovering mute woman in the room, who immediately exited stage right.

At last, Ravi thought. He crossed his leg over the other and felt the requisite pins and needles for the scene.

"I know where she is," said Lady Ivory, "and I think you're the only one who can bring her back."

"Where is she?"

"She's in the U.K. In London."

Well, I wonder how she knows that?

"How do you know?"

"Mr. Darcy tracked her down."

"What is your relationship to Leeza?"

"Let's just say, I was a friend of the woman who took responsibility for Leeza when she was a child. That friend has since deceased."

"And Mr. Darcy, the fixer? You hired him? You're behind all this Olsen Triplet stuff?"

"You should know, Ravi, I've kept this a secret for years myself—even from Lord Ivory, who often wondered why I would never miss an episode of *Full House,* even when it conflicted with *Charlie Rose.* My friend, Leeza's mother—at least, the only mother Leeza's ever known—was a wonderful woman. A dear friend, which, as far as concepts go, is as foreign to me as Flemish. I met her when we were both in our cabana-boy phase. I grew out of it; she never really did. Her life wasn't always the easiest, but she did everything she could for her daughter. I helped. Encouraged the girl's acting. And I always kept tabs on her. As you know, I've done well in the marriage department, but not so well in the realm of children. Leeza helped to fill the gap, one might say. The fact that she was a one-third was not uttered. And her mother waited until she was on her deathbed to tell her of her Olsen provenance. This was eight months ago."

Ravi could feel Lady Ivory's relief, the burden of secrets lifting. And then, just right then, she emitted something that came out something like this: "Yee yee ha ha yee yee ha-ha-ha." Hearing this beautiful chord of laughter, he thought, Well, here, clearly, is a woman with the rare humour and the intelligence to laugh at herself.

"Pardon me," she said, barely able to get out those words before breaking into more unchastened giggles. "It's the fish," she said, pointing to the basin in which her two feet fell.

Not waiting for an invitation, Ravi wandered over to see that there were, indeed, dozens of little swimmers going around in the tub. "Right. A fish pedicure. I think I saw Vanessa Williams getting this treatment on *Ugly Betty.*" He shrugged.

"*Garra rufa,*" murmured Lady Ivory. "That's the name of the fish. They nibble at the dead skin and gnaw away at the calluses. Started in Turkey, but I picked up the habit during a trip to Fiji. Very efficient."

"And laughter, after all, is the best medicine," added Ravi. He moved back to his appointed seat. "So, you were saying? Leeza found out only fairly recently that she's an Olsen and a triplet. And you've decided now's the time for this info to get out. Why?"

He wanted to say, What's in it for you?, but instead he phrased it: "And this will be beneficial to all parties, I suspect?"

Lady Ivory looked right at Ravi. Then she took her feet out of the basin in one effortless swoop. "I know how it feels to be marginalized, Ravi. I've seen it with this dark interlude in my husband's life. I see the looks. We've been tried in public. People we thought were friends have fled. In my own way, I understand what it might feel like to be the third Olsen sister."

Am I buying any of this?

"Leeza needs to have her moment in the sun, leave at long last her chrysalis. I owe her mother that much."

Oh, and you're not interested in Lotto Leeza?

"And just to clarify, Lady Ivory, for this moment in the sun . . . for this, you need me."

"She'll listen to you. Plus, I know you want to see this through. Don't you, Ravi?"

He stood up.

"Don't you?" she asked again, putting out one of her arms/tongs.

"Of course I do."

"I've read my history, and we are like Khrushchev and Mao in this particular escapade," she deviated now. "We may both have ideologies and goals, but we have to pull together. You go get the girl. I help my dearly departed friend. You get your story and a bit part in a drama. You also get to keep the sun off your deepest, darkest secret. Our girl, Leeza, gets her turn on stardom's seesaw."

And, you, Lady Ivory, you buy some insurance from me going forward in the social sphere because, as someone as savvy as you knows full well, I'm the kind of guy who's kindest to my sources.

Right on cue, she uttered, "Of course, what's a little social rehabilitation when you've got the biggest story of your career? Hypothetically speaking?"

Has the Lady lost her Edith Wharton marbles?

But the Lady had one more card up her sleeve, which she had theatrically saved for last.

"Oh, and this International Noël Coward/Oscar Wilde Fellowship you've applied for in Paris? The one you're so keen to land, two years, all expenses paid?"

His neck grew.

"I just happen to have a good friend on the selection committee." Jaunty pause. "You can get out of this racket, Ravi. Get to Paris. You can slide right in. But first the girl needs to be found."

It was Ravi's turn to look right at Lady Ivory. "London, you say?"

"That is correct."

He took out a slip of paper from his pocket and had a quick peek. It was the list he'd just procured of all the big parties happening in all the big cities. Lady Ivory watched him do so and then waited patiently for him to say something.

"By jolly, I've got it!" he began in an atrocious British accent. "I think I know just where I have to be."

And this time, Lady Ivory laughed all on her own.

20

"My Baby Just Cares for Me"

There were mini-shots of gazpacho hanging from trees, and waiters with morally pliable constitutions, and rafts of chaps who looked like modern-day Lord Byrons in porn-star sun specs.

For every titled playboy, there was a besotted damsel in an age-inappropriate garment, and for every PLRG (Poor Little Rich Girl, if you have to ask), there was the odd man who looked to be a gay gym receptionist. Making his circuitous way around the Savoy, in the Queen of England's hometown, Ravi was immediately thrown into the line of fire of one-and-two kisses on the cheek (even in England now, there was ample confusion about this), the precise pitter-patter of Slavic-splattered accents (when, oh when, had the London social scene become so Russian?), and the moving, never-ending tableau of masculine bedhead (what, oh what, had Jamie Oliver wrought?). Finally, there was the spectre of utter orthodontic wonderfulness (despite all the clichés, the new kids in the new London had overcome the dental failures of past generations).

Snatches of conversations rose up—"skiing in Cortina," "Stockholm Syndrome," "William and Kate," "curry and a pint"—as Ravi attempted to smoke out the place. He smiled at women who were clearly capital-T trouble, poured into bias-cut dresses. Crossed paths with yet another who looked like the British Bride of Vicodin. Took an Earl Grey–glazed samosa from one of the pin-sharp Lothario waiters, who, yes, oozed with moral pliability but also gave off the scent of Gender Reassignment Surgery. Offered up his best half-cocked grin to a publicist making the rounds.

"I think it's brilliant you could come out tonight," she said after a definitive double-kiss hi-how-are-you, hypnotizing him with her clipped diction. "The hotel just reopened, you know." He did, indeed. He also knew but was reminded now by her that the Savoy—once dubbed "the Palace by the Thames"—was as laurelled as you could get. And that its legendary blend of Edwardian design and art deco go-get-'em had lured everyone from Churchill to Winehouse over the years, and that its recent facelift constituted what was said to be Britain's Most Expensive Hotel Restoration Ever. He knew that Claude Monet painted here, that Oscar Wilde trysted here, that Alfred Hitchcock haunted here, that Bob Dylan recorded here. He knew that César Ritz (who would go on to found the Ritz Hotel) was the Savoy's first manager, and that Guccio Gucci—yes, *the* Gucci—once toiled as a bellboy here (humping all the Fancy People's luggage before realizing that he could make fancier luggage for them!). He knew that the Savoy was one of his must-stops in London.

"Did you know that Melba toast was invented at the Savoy?"

asked the publicist. Ravi mentally remarked that she had significant assets and was palpably more post-millennial Brigitte Bardot than she was run-of-the-mill Bridget Jones.

"I'd heard that," he answered. "And it's still true, isn't it, that the Savoy is the only place in London that you drive on the right, American-style, when entering the driveway?"

"Brilliant, isn't it?" she said.

"Well, if you'll excuse me, I have a friend to find," he ejected, getting back to the business at hand.

"Brilliant!" she adiosed.

And off he was, on his across-the-pond hunt. Approaching one of the gazpacho trees, he thought he had hit the j-a-c-k-p-o-t. Maybe it was too easy, but he swore he could see the outline of Leeza just steps away. She was in chiffon, and from behind he could see her dress foaming just so. "Leeza!" he began to say when suddenly his phone made a plea. It was his indomitable mother, with her sterling timing.

"Ravi?" she asked.

"Hi, Mummy," he said, trying not to lose the girl in chiffon and taking another samosa while he was at it.

"Ravi! You have brought shame to the family again."

"What did I do this time, Mummy?"

"My friends, they talk. They saw your picture in national magazine!"

"Oh," he whispered. "That sounds just horrible."

She kept talking. "I saw photo too. You look dark, too dark. You look like you work in farm."

"Mummy, I was in the Galapagos Islands interviewing a movie

star on her set right before that picture appeared in *HELLO!* magazine. It's a good thing! I was invited to interview Reese Witherspoon!"

"What is Galapagos?" she bellowed. "What is Witherspoon?"

"Never mind."

"Too dark, Ravi. Too dark." She was, by now, on the inevitable precipice of tears.

"Okay, Mummy, I promise not to go in the sun anymore. In fact, I'm in England, where there is no sun. Can I go now, though? I'm in the middle of something important."

Putting away his phone, he fumbled once again toward the beauty in chiffon. His fingers in play, he tapped the young thing on her shoulder. At which point, a woman who was not Leeza, had never been Leeza, turned her nose in a way that only a Brit, and in particular a Sloane Ranger, can do. And sniffed.

"I'm sorry," he managed, moving right along.

That's when he was pretty sure he heard another woman exclaim near him, "Oh my God! There are people with actual head wounds at this party! How chic!"

Yes. Head wounds. How could he forget? And how could he fail to take note of a great quote when he heard one? This playboy-heavy party, happening at the newly restored hotel, was, after all, in honour of the end of the latest Gumball Rally, an annual 3,000-mile auto race begun by an ex-Armani model named Maximillion Cooper (real name!), which never failed to draw a coterie of celebrities, genteels, and the odd throne-less royal. Essentially, it was a richy-rich auto race for daredevils, with shades of Jack Kerouac—one that travelled the world and had varying routes, year to year. Kate Moss had burned the rubber one year; so, too, had faux-lifeguard David Hasselhoff, faux-mermaid Daryl Hannah, and real skateboarder Tony Hawk. This year, the most fame-devouring frump of all time, belter Susan Boyle, was a special guest driver. Starting in Madrid, this latest rally routed through Marbella, Casablanca, Marrakesh, Fez, Barcelona, Paris, and now London. Six days. Five nights. Two hundred cars, including your requisite hodge-podge of Ferraris, Lamborghinis, Bentleys, and Rolls-Royces.

Ravi had attended a Gumball party in the south of France once, and had long thought it to be one of the unique tribal gatherings one could find. And if Leeza was in London—as he had been told—and she was at a party, there was no way she wasn't going to be at this one. For starters, it promised more than enough man-potential for a self-denying celebrity like our Leeza.

Now, if only he could find her!

He was dabbling still on his ongoing search when he encountered Adrien Brody. Looking very racy race-car driver, he was in tight white jeans and a black leather jacket over a tank top, with a supersized silver chain. He was standing next to Susan Boyle, and, naturally, he was waxing eloquent about his own Gumball experience. Ravi thought he heard the word *freedom* a few times. Getting closer, he extracted the following direct quote from the skinny, ballerina-hipped Oscar winner: "I think everyone wants a certain freedom within certain parameters."

Taking precise mental notes, he made small talk with a wayward preppy from Belgium, sent an unrequited air kiss to It Girl Peaches Geldof, and then decided to tailgate the curvaceous (but not as curvaceous as she used to be) model/writer Sophie Dahl, who was famous for once having dallied with Mick Jagger and for being the granddaughter of the guy who wrote *Charlie and the Chocolate Factory.*

Would that she could lead him to Leeza. If Sophie was anywhere as good with plot as her granddad, maybe, just maybe, she could help to move this one along.

Sophie, dressed in one of those all-the-rage boyfriend jackets, was heading out of the main lobby of the hotel and up a small flight of stairs. Ravi stayed with her. On his way, he passed Camilla Al-Fayed, whose Harrods-owning, royal-family-fighting dad had not stopped her from achieving heroine status in London, and then one of the non-age-defying lust objects from Duran Duran. Taking swift gazelle-like steps, Sophie, dear Sophie, led him to the grandmama of all cocktail lounges, a.k.a. the American Bar. The natural home of the dry martini, the intimate, horseshoe-sized bar was famously but not flashily grand and, as always, theatrically hushed. Perfect black and white photos of luminaries covered the walls, including one of Elizabeth Taylor putting what they call a fag in David Bowie's mouth, and another of Bogart and Bacall, looking tentative but together. F. Scott Fitzgerald, Bing Crosby, Rita Hayworth, you name it, they were all there, frozen in photo-time.

Often known as one of the great bars in all the world, this spot had not been touched in the Savoy's restoration because, well, the American Bar was its own icon and never became a designosaurus. And, here, now, in the belly of this deco beast, right near an unfeasibly beautiful piano, sat the young woman who had been on his mind. He recognized her fingers before he saw her because there she was sitting with a gentleman caller with a head wound, and she was air-quoting with great abandon.

"Cheers, Leeza, with a zed," interrupted Ravi, going right up to his friend seated on a tooth-shaped stool. Someone was playing Nina Simone's "My Baby Just Cares for Me" on the piano.

"What if I said I wasn't?" she asked. Her gentleman friend grinned, exuding an Etonian warmth.

"Bollocks, my darling," Ravi said, pulling up a molar stool of his own. "Don't be coy. I've come all the way across the ocean to find you, so you could at least pretend to be happy to see me." Tick-tock, tick-tock went Ravi's mental stopwatch. "So, Leeza, tell me. Have you by any chance ever tried a fish pedicure?"

21

A Sharp Left at Anderson Cooper

In the end, after Ravi had unloaded his uncommon powers of persuasion, Leeza did relent. And did decide to let her neck be bitten by the fangs of fame. But she had, first, a request.

"Wait, where did you say she said?" asked Rory when he called to give her the 411.

"The diva-in-training is all for making her Tripletness official, but she also says that her heart tells her she needs to see Ashley and Mary-Kate one more time before she does anything."

"What?" Ravi could pretty much see Rory's eyes squinting like Richard Gere's.

"It was her one condition. After I found her at the Savoy, we went off to the Wolseley for breakfast-as-dinner, which is when Leeza told me feels she needs to be in a room with them, and just look at them, look deep into their eyes—not necessarily talk to them—to summon up the inner strength to go through with all this. She calls it a 'doorway' she needs to go through before she heads into the 'main atrium' of her task. I think she took to reading *The Kite Runner* or something during her disappearance because I don't remember her being so mystical."

"Well, how deeply, strangely engrossing," replied Rory, dry as an extra-dry martini. "But how'd you convince her when you found her in London? Tell me everything, Ravi, but tell me in one hundred words or less."

"I basically convinced her that she had an 'appointment with destiny,'" said Ravi.

"And what, pray tell, else?"

"One word. Four letters. S-W-A-G."

"Oh, you took my advice."

"Of course I took your advice, my beautiful baklava. I went over in excruciating detail all the free things she'd be missing out as a celebrity, whatever bracket of celebrity she eventually falls into. Even as the Other Olsen Sister—"

"So to speak," rushed in Rory.

"So to speak," he intoned, going on to say, "Even as the so-called Other Olsen Sister, she'd be in hot demand and privy to any number of things. The prospect of free clothes, free trips, and free plasma screens spoke to our young Leeza. I had brought along with me that PowerPoint presentation you came up with listing the myriad opportunity costs, in regards to swag, so thank you. It worked . . ."

"Like a charm?" assisted Rory.

"So to speak." It was Ravi's turn to intone.

After which, Rory asked him, "So, does Leeza seem at all different?"

"Well, she has bangs now."

"Oh, I see."

They both laughed.

She picked up. "So what now? What's the end-game here?"

"Start spreading the news," he began to half-sing.

"What?"

"We're in New York now. On Fifth Avenue, in fact, as you and I dialogue."

"Why?"

"If Leeza can make it here, she can make it anywhere! No, seriously, the Olsen Twins—so to speak—are in New York right now, I just happen to know—"

"So, you're plotting a chance encounter with Leeza's dear sisters."

"It's already lined up," he replied while passing the big glass shrine to Apple, just steps away from the famous kiddyland cathedral, FAO Schwartz, and just a traffic stop away from where *The Way We Were* played out. Oh, the Plaza!

"Ravi?" she asked, feeling a New York reverie coming on. "Ravi? Are you there?"

"Yes, sorry. As I was saying, I suggested we come to New York lickety-split because tonight's the annual *Time* magazine party. Y'know, that big one I go to every year, in honour of the Hundred Most Influential People in the World?"

"And you're telling me those dwarfettes have been chosen for that list? Gimme a break. What, was neither Jane Goodall nor Steve Jobs available?"

"No, it's not like that. Y'know how they like to throw in some fashion to go along with all the billionaires, movie stars, and okey-dokey inventors, well, that really hot designer, Camus, he's on this year's list, and Ashley and Mary-Kate have been asked to introduce him at the dinner."

"So, you're going to take her to this *Time* thing, and Olsen Number Three is going to look at Olsen Numbers One and Two, after which Olsen Number Three is going to locate her inner strength, and then you're going to bring her back to Toronto and all is going to be okay? Is that your exit strategy?"

"More or less," he said, breathing in. "And by the way, you sexy serpent you, I love the fact that you just used the term *exit strategy.*"

"How'd you get to New York so fast anyway?" Rory asked. "Weren't you in London just a few hours ago?"

"Well, we absolutely had to get to this party. Remember Jason Doughton?"

"Mr. Big-Bucks Eligible Bachelor? The one who you caught with his mistress in Gaytown all those years ago, but you never breathed a word?"

"Yes, he happened to be in London, and I happened to run into him at the Wolseley."

"Let me guess—"

"He wasn't averse to lending us his private plane, let's just say."

What a blaze of hubris it was just a few hours later! So popped the scene when Ravi and Leeza walked into the Time Warner Center, stepping into an elevator that would eventually take them into a wedding-cake-staired convention room and, before that, into a dusky cocktail room, which was generic except for its gang. It was a lesson he'd learned from years and years of partygoing: people are always the best decor. And this decor, to be precise, was made up of the many who came with seat-fillers at various award shows, mixing ably with those whose quotes had appeared on the sides of Starbucks cups.

The notable notes of ambition hit Ravi almost as soon as he stepped to the bar behind *The Simpsons'* Matt Groening, found elbowing the man who had created the Human Genome Project. Besides the billionaires, movie stars, designers, and world-go-'round mogul inventors, there were any number of rock icons, sports legends, and media biggies in the room, all of whom were assessing the field and keeping the score. People who were too famous to carry business cards—it would be a little stalkerish to even ask for one—went about merrily self-editing, all the while mentally calculating their place vis-á-vis.

It was all like lard to the gossip columnist, of course. And even though *Vanity Fair*'s annual Oscar party, held in L.A., was probably more famous, more lauded, and, well, more outwardly glamorous, this *Time* affair was as much of a "get" but arguably more power-padded and with more of a mix.

"Isn't that Queen Noor?" asked Leeza when Ravi returned from ferrying drinks. She looked like she had teleported back to 1983 to get the magenta off-the-shoulder thing she had on. It did not not stand out here, in a sweeping hall full of a few hundred people at the most. Her flair for costuming was no less, but Leeza did seem a little more—how could he put it?—centred. The time off had evidently been good for her.

"Yes," he confirmed, handing her a glass. "And that's Martha Stewart over there. She gets the prize for being at this schmooze-a-palooza every year since *Time* started it a few years back. Hasn't missed one. Oprah, on the other hand, gets the prize for being on the list every year but only making it once. She usually just sends Gayle."

"So have you seen them?" asked wide-eyed Leeza, changing the topic to her famous sisters.

"I haven't. But they will be here. It's early still. Most of the name celebrities seem to arrive after the thinkers and the scientists. See that spiritually rich woman over there? She wrote *Eat, Pray, Love.* Oh, and there's Donald Trump!"

The cotton-candy-haired tycoon, whom Ravi had never met, shouted to him as he passed by, "Hey, man, how you doin'?" And while this may have seemed unusual, it wasn't really because in a room like this a certain clubbiness comes with just being invited. It was customary for people to either a) pretend to know others or b) make the mistake of knowing people they didn't.

"Well, thanks for getting me in," said Leeza.

"Oh, you're welcome. I had to pull a few strings, and they don't have a seat for you at dinner, but it's all good. By next year, you'll be the one getting me in to parties, I'm sure." He winked. "I'm just happy that you're here. I was worried that you really might have disappeared altogether."

Leeza looked deeply, fabulously touched, then said, "I was just so scared before, Ravi, but I'm in tune with inner warriorness now. I just need to see them once. Really look at them before they find out. I think it will help set my, like, ki."

"I think it's chi," mumbled Ravi, as Ms. *Eat, Pray, Love* crossed their path to get to John Mayer, who was standing beside Henry Kissinger.

Soon they were coming fast and furious. Money maven Suze Orman! Motormouth Chris Rock! Sultan of Sarcasm Jon Stewart! Non-starving artist Jeff Koons! So many Masters of the Universe, and so many of them with their de rigueur second or third Asian wives! Leeza kept looking for their targets, and Ravi kept looking at her looking. He was a little nervous, if he were to be a little honest with himself.

A roar went up when Aurora Kidd walked in, putting in nonverbal terms what happens when a star—an actual star—walks in among people who are just as, if not more, accomplished but lack that practised thing called presence. Posing like her life depended on it—an effortless effort, if there was such a thing—she lit the place up and even got the attention from a world-famous epidemiologist, who looked like your average trigonometry professor who secretly works for Interpol. His camera-phone was working overtime. But then popped up a white-sari-wrapped Aishwarya Rai, the Indian actress who's sometimes called the Most Beautiful Woman in the World. Aurora gave her scene-stealer a non-sanitary look, and then Harvey Weinstein, the famous boss-man to the stars, appeared by her side and, ignoring the previous star, said to Rai, "We're going to Cipriani later. Come."

"After-party at Cipriani," Ravi now mouthed to Leeza, having spent years honing his crackerjack eavesdropping. She turned her head and looked, to him, pretty much ready to cry, barf, and pass out all at once.

"You see them, don't you?" he said, looking across the black-tie sea.

Leeza managed a nod but not much more. He took her arm and headed for those long-losts. "I know this is emotional," he said, stomping past the actual Craig from Craigslist and taking a sharp left at Anderson Cooper. "But you can do this, Leeza. You can. They're not any better than you. You all come from the same place, don't forget."

He stopped for a second and poked Leeza. "There may be two of them, but you're twice the person they are. You got it, kid?"

She managed another nod and then added a whimper.

"You got it?" he repeated, sergeant-like. "Leeza?"

"I got it," she finally said.

"Okay then, let's do it," he said. "There's no time like this present *Time* party."

They made a circle, crisscrossing a war hero cooling his heels and making a beeline for a minor revolutionary, beside whom stood the two iconic, in-the-money Olsens. Mary-Kate, as usual, was the one who looked like she had dressed in the dark. Suze Orman was standing there too, as it happens, and Ravi could hear her giving them financial advice. So riveted by her investment strategies were they that they barely noticed Leeza. Leeza, though, stopped right in front of them and, letting her inner warriorness come through, stared into them like they were the mirrors that they were. Ashley noticed the girl staring and proceeded to give her a look that was vaguely sorrowful.

Leeza looked at them, and they both looked at her, and a frequency passed between them. Ravi saw the charge for himself;

could really feel it. The moment, which sat like a millennium, eventually passed, and then Leeza walked off into the distance, or at least toward the bar. "So?" asked Ravi, catching up to her. "So?"

She looked at him, and then he looked at her, and he knew. The tension in Leeza's shoulders had lessened palpably.

"Let's get those bitches," she said. "It's about time."

"Ravi?"

"Hello?'

"Ravi, it's Richard Johnson."

"Oh, hey, Richard. What's up?" What was the dashing, all-powerful editor of "Page Six," the world's most important gossip column, doing calling him at this hour? It was near midnight. He and Richard often traded bilateral scoops, and when Ravi had first begun doing his column, he'd been flattered when some people had started calling him "the Richard Johnson of Canada."

"How was the *Time* thing?" asked his fellow muckraker.

"Not bad. I thought I would have seen you at it, actually," replied Ravi.

"No, not this year. I was on kid patrol tonight," he said, pausing uncomfortably. "Listen, Ravi, we have a story in tomorrow's paper, and I just wanted to give you the courtesy of knowing, mano a mano, gossip to gossip."

"What do you mean?" asked Ravi.

"It's about the Olsen Twins," said Richard. "We got a hot tip about this story. Fuckin' unbelievable. We've heard that there's a third sister—and that you were with her last night. Or so my sources tell me . . ."

"Wait, what are you trying to say, Richard?"

"Well, something tells me you've been sitting on this story, and, well . . ." The voice at the other end stalled. "Well, Ravi, my friend, as you also know, it's all fair in love and tattle. We're running the bombshell about the Olsen Triplets. It hits 'Page Six' tomorrow."

22

Easy, Breezy

There's nothing a red carpet abhors more than dead space. As Leeza inched her way up a crimson trail, simpering knowingly, people clapped their hands like they were at Sea World. The photogs, lined up as far as the eye could see, shot and shot and shot—like it was a lunar landing. Or, more likely, the Third Coming. Slowly, she walked, steely yet winsome. The insinuation of a secret. Big smile.

Her sisters weren't far behind.

"Talk about a three-ring circus!" remarked Rory, looking on with Ravi from behind the barricades.

"I'm so incredibly proud of her. I really am," quivered her husband.

"Oh, Ravi. You're getting so sappy, trees for miles are going to be jealous!"

"I'm hardly one to talk, but someone may just have to revoke your analogy licence."

The scene, here at the entrance of Roy Thomson Hall, was

extra-effusive, even for a time of year in Toronto when extra-effusive is the norm, movie premieres are constant, and stars fall to the streets the way subscription cards tumble out of *Vanity Fair.* It was the Toronto International Film Festival, unspooling only a few months after the Greatest Triplet Scandal of All Time had rocked the planet.

"Leeza! Leeza!" That was Ravi calling. That was Leeza not turning. That was Goldie and Kurt Russell floating past them, fresh as daisies after a late-season stint at their cottage up north.

As the photogs scurried, and a village-sized cast of fans held out their palms, Ravi and Rory watched as one male equerry guided Leeza by hand, another one paced right behind her, and yet another—an elegant yet stern-looking older buffer-lady—worked the press line to designate who would speak to her and when.

"I don't think she can hear you," empathized Rory.

"Oh, look, she's holding a Moleskine," stage-whispered an even prouder Ravi, taking in the mysteriously black notebook that Leeza clutched. It accessorized her just-rolled-out-of-bed look, consisting of a half-open oversized white shirt and black stockings enlivened by the steepest of Bruno Frisonis. In a red-carpet world of mermaid tails and prom-time silhouettes, the get-up did, indeed, stand out. It was not too studied but just contrived enough.

Well, kiddo, Ravi thought to himself, taking Rory's hand, you lost the scoop, but you won the girl.

"Leeza! Leeza!" tried Rory, her exclamations fading fast into the overall chorus.

After the Robert Frostian two-roads-diverged-in-a-wood

Time magazine event, when Mr. "Page Six" had called to say that he had the Leeza story, Ravi, inevitably, panicked. It was the insatiable scoopmeister in him. For a few minutes, he thought about outwitting "Page Six." Or at least out-tweeting. He was all set to save the story for himself by putting the critical info out in a 140-word capsule on Twitter. But just as he was about to, his fingers had stalled at Send.

Taking in a few yogic breaths, Ravi had scrapped the thought. The truth, then as now, was that he was a gossip traditionalist and he wanted Leeza to have her place in the sun—in an actual newspaper, not online! Plus, he'd considered in that luxury hotel room, after travelling that long and wonky road with Leeza, perhaps this was the universe's way of telling him it was time to leave, at long last, the party. He wanted out of the gossip racket, after all—go to Paris on his fellowship, write novels, live in holy man-and-woman matrimony with Rory—so maybe this was his chance.

By the next day, the news was out, and all the expected tremors were felt. The putrid stew of rumour and speculation began, disappeared, and came back again. Instantly, Leeza was a star, with Mary-Kate and Ashley getting a nice famelift too. They were on the front covers of mags for weeks and weeks. Larry and Barbara and Oprah weighed in. In Canada, George Stroumboulopoulos on the CBC devoted an unruly hour to the three united sisters. Sanjay Gupta on CNN weighed in with a scientific special on triplets. Unsurprisingly, Marc Jacobs named a bag after the new Olsen, famed trainer-to-the-stars Harley Pasternak began pumping with her, *Sesame Street* cordially invited her on the show a cappella with the Cookie Monster, and CoverGirl, soon enough, got her saying, "Easy, Breezy" in her own hair commercial. The girl even managed to appear as a clue in the venerable *New York Times* crossword! Overnight, too, celeb mecca Kitson, in L.A., began selling tees in packs of three—each one featuring a different triplet mug.

Though the original two sisters—"Vintage Olsen," as some of the tabs had begun calling them—were a little circumspect at first, and even a little hostile, things warmed up just as soon as it became clear what a celebrity (and cash) boon this was. Although Mary-Kate and Ashley's big-screen fortunes weren't exactly wilting before all this went down, now scripts were pouring in pretty much every day. David Cronenberg wanted them for what he called his creepy triplet trilogy. Various movies were in negotiations, including a ready remake called *The Three Stoogettes.*

These negotiations, plus the ever-ready allure of swag—nobody loved free stuff more than celebs who could readily afford it—had brought the girls to the all-important festival in Toronto.

"Ravi, is that you?" called out someone in the crowd. Someone on the right side of the barricades. "What are you doing behind there?"

"Oh, hi, Tripp," Ravi greeted sheepishly. Tripp was the guy who'd replaced Ravi on the gossip beat for the *National Mirror,* after Ravi had oh-so-graciously bowed out. Tripp was all the rage. Tripp was drowning in invites. Tripp never had a night in.

"Seriously, Ravi, it's so weird to see you back there!" he went on. "Oh, how the mocha-skinned have fallen!" he added, chuckling at his own cleverness.

"Well, it's what happens when you retire," he rejoined. "We're off to Paris tomorrow," he said, gesturing at Rory, "but we wanted to see our girl," pointing to Leeza.

"Actually, I don't think we've formally met," said Tripp, showing off his soap-opera leading-man white smile and a small orange filter of powder above his upper lip. He extended his hand to Rory. "Behind every faux-gay man there is a woman, isn't there?" he said, chuckling again.

"Nice to meet you, Tripp," said Rory, taking his hand. "I've heard a lot about you."

The news of Ravi's true sexual provenance—which had followed the news of Leeza's tripletness—had provided much in-town fodder for jokes.

"Who ever heard of a *straight* gossip columnist?" asked one magazine in a snarky aside about the matter. "Not that there's anything wrong with not being gay!" cracked Jason Kevins, the tamarind-toned funnyman, who had a new act that used it all for grist. "Wait, you're straight?" asked his own editor, Sam. "With *that* hair?"

"Nice to meet you too," said Tripp to Rory, who was smiling the smile of a woman whose husband had stopped phoning in his spousal performance.

"Well, I gotta get inside," shifted Tripp. "Penelope Cruz and Salma Hayek are saving me a seat!" As he disappeared into the boiling red-carpet tableau, a royal roar went up when Cinder-Leeza, as yet another tab had begun calling her, stopped to fervently pose with Mary-Kate and Ashley. It was quite the scene. A big, bad brouhaha of Bright Young Things!

Cojo, the Canada-sprung contortionist, lunged at them with his *Entertainment Tonight* mic, giving an uncanny Carly Simon in the process.

"Wait," exclaimed Rory. "Isn't that . . . ?" She nodded toward the woman standing next to Leeza. The stern-looking woman, with her hair in a taut chignon, decked head to toe in designer-ready security-guard black, clipboard in hand, was strangely, oddly, familiar. It was Lady Ivory! She was the professional buffer-lady! And noticing Ravi and Rory and their slack-jawed stares, the beautifully appointed buffer-lady waved happily.

"She looks pretty good out there," said another voice, sidling up behind them. It was a voice that came with a sweater vest. "Lady Ivory says she's having the ride of her life with Leeza."

"They both look pretty good," said Ravi.

"How wonderful to see you again, Mr. Darcy," greeted Rory.

"Ditto," he said.

"Here for the big show?" inquired Ravi.

"All's well that ends well," said Mr. Darcy, ably mixing his Austen with his Shakespeare. "Want to beat this joint and grab some Bloody Caesars?" he followed up. "I know a good place."

"I thought you'd never ask," replied the gossip emeritus.

"Sounds perfect," said Rory.

Gathering themselves, the trio prepared to ditch the celebrity shenanigans when Leeza ejected herself mid-photo-op and ran over to the three familiars lurking beyond the red carpet. "Ravi! Rory! Mr. Darcy!"

"Congratulations, Leeza," said Rory. "I just love your stockings."

"You done good, my girl," beamed Mr. Darcy.

Ravi, his emotional reserve overruled, extended his arms and moved in tighter than Shirley MacLaine to Debra Winger in *Terms of Endearment*. Then, hug complete, he dug into the left breast pocket of his Canali-sponsored herringbone sports jacket and pulled out two pieces of paper. One was the acceptance letter for the two-year, all-expenses-paid International Noël Coward/Oscar Wilde Fellowship. The other was the one-way ticket for their flight to Paris the next day.

He waved these two things in the air with a smile and a lone teardrop stalking his cheek, eliciting an all-natural squeal from Leeza. He didn't say anything. He couldn't. For once, Ravi was at a loss for words.

Acknowledgements

All the world's a party, and all the men and women merely sources. But some are more than just. And they're the ones that made this book—and my trajectory—possible. My parents, Mansoor and Laila Govani, to whom this book is dedicated, braved a language (and serious weather) gap to bring me to this country as a kid. We were refugees, fleeing, flummoxed. Who knew back then that their baby would transition into a social arbiter of sorts, and that I would one day be mingling with the very people I grew up watching on the tube, peering at pictures of in magazines. Alice, meet Wonderland.

Shout-outs: to my sister, Rishma, and her husband, Alykhan, and their son, Khalil, for their support and encouragement, and for "getting me." To Ann Layton, for giving me a continual respite in Barbados, and for her perspicacity on all occasions. To Bobby Dhillon, for lending me his place in Belize one summer, where much of the stirrings for this novel began. To Russia, where—during another part of the same fateful summer—this novel really began to make sense as well as take shape! To Natalie Kovacs, the best Funny Girl I know—someone who really puts the *bon* in *vivant.* To Amber Malik, for the ongoing hi-jinks and the *que sera sera.* To Ben

Errett, Maryam Siddiqi, and Sarah Murdoch for having my back—and making me look good! To Dominick Dunne, who psychically nudged me in so many ways! To Jennifer Lambert, my eagle-eyed editor at HarperCollins, who has not an ounce of Devil in her Prada, and who was an indubitable joy to work with every step of the way. To the entire tireless team at HarperCollins, and to my agent, Sam Hiyate, for his amiable mixing of business and pleasure. To Nicholas Mellamphy, for his patience, intuition, and clemency.